ROSÉ IN SAINT TROPEZ

Also by Mike Attebery

On/Off – A Jekyll & Hyde Story
Billionaires, Bullets, Exploding Monkeys
Seattle On Ice
Bloody Pulp

ROSÉ IN SAINT TROPEZ

a novella by

Mike Attebery

Cryptic Bindings

Seattle

Rosé in Saint Tropez

Cryptic Bindings, LLC.
Visit our website: www.crypticbindings.com
Read Mike Attebery's blog: www.mikeattebery.com

First Edition: November 2015

ISBN: 978-0-692-49938-2

Publisher's Note:
This is a work of fiction. Names, characters, places, and incidents are either the product of the author's imagination or are used fictitiously, any resemblance to actual persons (living or dead), business establishments, events, or locales is coincidental.

Printed in the United States of America.

For the people who made my
childhood summers unforgettable.

New York

He could hear them out in the darkness.

Murmuring.

Waiting for his return.

This was the part of tonight's show, the part of *every* show that he truly savored. The fleeting moments before the encore, when the cheers died down, the lights stayed low, and he could *feel* the energy in the air as it wafted over him, awash with the smells of liquor and dancing, perfume and smoldering joints.

At the start of the night, before he and the band stepped out on stage, before the first song, he still got that swimming feel in the pit of his stomach. Nerves and anxiety. Pent up adrenaline. Some frontmen still threw up backstage. He'd talked to a few of them, *big names*, who'd told him in confidence that even now, decades into their careers, they still let the nervous energy get the better of them. Will had gotten past that point after the first couple of years, but in the beginning he'd been unbearably shy whenever he was pushed into the spotlight. Now he just had the briefest moment's hesitation before he strummed the opening chords, closed his eyes, and let loose the first lyrics. After that, each performance drifted by in a sort of daze, like a strange dream in which he sang and danced, the audience cheered, and Will and his bandmates played together in perfect balance, speeding up the tempo, pausing, shifting up the keys, and swapping parts. One musician after another stepped into center stage while the rest of the group backed him up. Then they'd work around again until Will Baker, he of the band's namesake, was once again at the microphone, wrapping up the latest set, thanking the crowd for their years of enthusiastic support, and leading the band offstage.

That's when the bandstands would start to rumble. The concrete floors would begin to shake. The cheers and applause would rise from the crowd, roll across the arena in waves, and roar down from the rafters overhead.

The moment he was out of sight back stage, a tour hand would pass Will a bottle of water. He'd take several long drinks, pour some of the cold water over his head, and quickly change out of his sweat-soaked shirt. All the while, the crowd would be cheering, hoping for an encore. If need be, he'd slip out for a piss, maybe take a drag off a smoke. A few more sips of water, a chat with the boys about what to play next, then the lights would dim, the band would walk out on stage, and the spotlight would spark back to life.

And then, like now, *here* at *Madison Square Garden* in New York City, stood Will Baker. He was 30-years-old, with five o'clock shadow, a thin, six-foot frame, scruffy, receding hair, and a guitar slung over his shoulder. If you saw him on the street, you'd pay him no mind. Dismiss him as a hired hand, or the bartender that he'd once been. But somehow, through some twist of cosmic fate that Will Baker above all others still found hysterical, he'd become a rock star. A rock star with screaming fans and more money than he could fathom.

Will looked out into the sea of dimly lit but beaming faces, breathed in the smells of the late summer crowd – the smoke and sweat and weed and beer – and tipped the microphone stand back toward him.

"Thank you very much, everybody," he said in his signature smoke-burnished drawl. "I hope you're all having a pleasant evening, hanging out with us tonight, the last night of our tour."

Will grinned as the crowd erupted in a fresh volley of screams.

"We really appreciate you coming out here in the middle of your busy work week to hear us tinkering with some tunes."

This was followed by more shouting and hollering as the crowd caught its collective breath and started in on round two.

"We sincerely appreciate it. We sincerely do. Thank you. Thank you. Thank you. Thank you. Thank you."

Will glanced back at the band. Nick – the oldest and most shy member of the group – was on sax, standing in the shadows of stage left, hiding behind Steve – the youngest member – who stood with his bass up front by the crowd. Parker – who was right around Will's age – was off to his right, a violin pressed under his chin. And then there was Chet in the back, drumsticks held high, a broad smile stretched out across his face. Chet was in his mid-forties, and like so many drummers before him, he acted in an unofficial capacity as the band's beating heart. At this point in the evening, most drummers would have been worn out, more than ready to call it a night, but aside from the sweat that trickled from Chet's brow, he looked utterly relaxed, seemingly prepared to perform another set.

He and Will locked eyes.

Chet nodded.

"This last song is about a girl that left me," Will murmured into the mic.

The crowd started booing.

"Kicked my ass to the curb."

The band began teasing their instruments. Lone notes echoed through the auditorium, rising and falling as the crowd grew quiet.

"No. No. I know what you're thinking. Not *that* girl," Will continued as his voice was drowned out by the audience's laughter. "This is a song about a girl from a long, *long* time ago. A girl that *mattered*." He shrugged his shoulders. "And she *still* got away."

His fingers started tickling the strings as he closed his eyes and let out a long, low grumble. He held the note, felt it swelling in his lungs. Someone in the back of the arena, a guy – it was *always* the guys – seemed to suspect what was coming next, and shouted his approval.

"We love you, Will!"

This was followed by a few catcalls.

Will paid them no mind. His thoughts were on the song, the sounds, the memories in his head that he had to draw upon if he wanted to do the number justice. This was one of the fans' favorites, one of the band's favorites too -- the tale of a holiday gone horribly wrong -- but it was a song that always ripped up his voice for days afterwards, which was why he very rarely sang it anymore. Plus, someone had told him it was time to move on. Maybe they were right. These days it was more of a tour closer, but this year, though the folks in the crowd couldn't possibly know why, it struck him as a more appropriate choice than ever. The crowd seemed to enjoy listening to Will as he poured his guts out, letting loose with a raw, wailing, angry roar, the kind of sounds that can only come from a man who knows was it's like to have his heart ripped out.

The crowd was loving it, as he knew they would. Catharsis is a funny thing. He'd written this number as a young man, when he was trying his damnedest to pull himself up from the wreckage of a romantic entanglement gone awry, but even as he'd been trudging along through the depths of his own despair, he'd been giving voice to the feelings of spurned lovers, men and women, the world over.

Will's eyebrows arched sporadically as he scanned the crowd, only fleetingly conscious of the words emanating from his mouth, of the motions his fingers were making over the strings.

Their fans danced and screamed and wailed into the darkness and swirling lights, until Will and the boys reached the crashing conclusion, the lights went down, and the crowd went wild.

Will made his way offstage. Nick and Parker followed close behind. Steve and Chet lingered on the stage, tossing out picks and sticks. At 25, Steve was the youngest member of the group, and he was just starting to soak in the glow of his own personal fame. He wandered the foot of the stage, slapping hands and flirting with girls. As for Chet, he just loved to joke with the crowd. He always walked to the front after a show to say something to his own personal fan-base, which was largely comprised of heavy-set guys in hockey jerseys with "Chet Barker" silk-screened across the backs.

Will walked down a ramp past the crowds of fans who'd either won radio contests for backstage passes, or donated a shitload of money to his favorite pet causes – be they environmental foundations or political action groups – with the reward being the chance to meet him and the boys after a show. The crowd was largely comprised of college kids, with a few folks in their twenties and thirties mixed in, their slightly sheepish expressions vanishing the moment they made eye contact with one of the band members. Will smiled and nodded. He shook hands, gave high fives, and signed a few album covers and T-shirts. Then, the next thing he knew, he and the band had slipped through a doorway and were holed up in the middle of a room full of banged up couches and chairs, surrounded by crew members, managers, personal assistants, and various relatives; wives, parents, children, and cousins.

Will was suddenly all too aware that he was the only one there without someone waiting for him. No sooner did the thought pop into his head, than it was knocked away by Chet's welcome interruption.

"That was a good fuckin' show. When you went into the first part of *Mischief Night*, I was just thinking '*fuck it,*' we haven't played that in ages."

Will blinked and shook his head. "And I think I proved

why."

"Nah, it was good man, it was good. Maybe not our best turn at it, but-"

"I liked it," Steve interrupted. "It was the perfect closer."

"Good tour." Parker said.

"*Great* tour." Chet corrected. "Definitely in the top three. I can't wait to get back in the studio."

"Just a few months from now, man," Will said. "Lets enjoy our summer and see where we're at in October."

The guys continued laughing and breaking down the performance song by song. Someone cracked open a few cases of Red Hook and passed the bottles around the room. They clinked the necks together and talked some more, gradually splintering off into their own little groups. Will watched Chet pick up his little girl and prop her up on his shoulders as he leaned forward and gave his wife a kiss. Parker stood off in the corner with his girlfriend. Nick and his fiancé were sitting on a couch talking quietly. Will smiled a bit wistfully as he noticed the two innocently holding hands.

The night and the beer flowed into the late hours, and the crowd slowly filtered away along with it, as one by one the band members and their various entourages departed for their hotels. Before they left, each of the boys slapped Will on the back and promised to stay in touch in the months between now and October. In the early days that would have gone without saying, but now, between tours and their increasingly sporadic recording studio forays, that was often easier said than done, as family and relationships ate up an ever-increasing portion of their off time.

Eventually, the only folks left in the room were Will and his various associates and business managers. There was Caroline, his personal assistant, a young woman of 26, who had been keeping his life in order for the last four years. She'd come to work for him right out of college, and had quickly become indispensable. She was cute, with medium length hair and a laugh that never failed to make him smile. She was his closest friend on the tour, or anywhere really. Will had made a conscious effort to keep things purely professional between them, if only out of fear of fucking up the one relationship in his life that seemed to work. He couldn't imagine functioning without her now.

The other folks in the room were his manager Larry, a big, well-fed man in his late fifties, with a pompadour of white hair, and the ability to talk his client into just about any business venture or musical expedition. Larry had picked the boys out at a bar gig more than a decade earlier and led them down the road to fame. If Will's lifestyle and success could be credited to one man, that man would be Larry. Larry was a buddy, to a degree, but there was always an element of business at work there, even if they were traveling together on holiday.

Last of all, there was Bobby, a heavy set guy with a goatee and a poker face, who managed Will's cash and investments, bought his properties, paid the taxes, and kept the books. He didn't do all of this entirely on his own, Will had learned enough from experience and the mistakes of others – he'd seen that *Behind the Music* episode on Billy Joel – to have all of his accounts and dealings audited regularly, but in the end, he trusted Bobby, and knew that if anyone could keep his financial house in order, he was the guy.

Will finished his last beer and started getting his stuff together. He had a long trip ahead of him, and as usual, the final day of the tour – filled with early radio interviews and last minute media appearances – had been a slog. It was starting to catch up with him. Unfortunately, all too often the hours after a tour were also when his three go-to people all seemed to have something they needed to discuss with him at the same time. Yet even as they jostled for Will's attention, their cell phones were ringing with messages and business decisions that demanded their immediate attention. Will stood in the middle of the room, trying to filter out the noise as he zipped his guitar into a padded shoulder bag.

"Your flight leaves at one," Caroline said. "You need to hit the road in the next few minutes."

Will nodded, even as Larry cut in.

"Now, don't forget, the folks upstairs need to know if you can make it to that solo show in August."

"Tell them I'm on vacation, Larry."

"They're really hoping-"

"We'll see where we are then," Will said, falling back on his most common procrastination answer. Larry nodded his head, knowing all too well what it meant. Will would be there.

There was a knock on the door and a young guy with a shaved head leaned in.

"Mr. Baker, there's a car here for you."

Will smiled. "Thank you."

"He'll be out in a minute," Caroline said.

Will glanced around the room and focused on his business manager.

"Bobby, you haven't gotten a word in yet."

"We'll go over the books when you get back," Bobby began. "Just keep in mind one thing..."

And yet, Will's mind was beginning to wander. After months on the road, and dozens upon dozens of cities, his brain was fried. His body was tired. His emotions were drained. He needed something stronger than beer, something warm and amber, with hints of oak and smoke and a burning aftertaste. If there was time, he'd grab a drink at the airport, if there wasn't, he'd have to hold out a little longer, and savor what he could get on the plane.

This vacation was much needed, even if it came under less than ideal circumstances. It had been far, far too long since he'd seen the whole crowd, reconnected with a few of his favorites, and had a taste of life away from the views and vices of the road, where anything seemed to go, but none of it *ever* seemed to matter, not in the right way at any rate.

Will's associates' voices were still murmuring around him, layering upon one another, addressing unfinished business, reassuring him, reminding him of commitments and, to some degree, justifying their pay. But he had stopped listening. It had all become just so much noise. Life and the tour had reached the saturation point, and it was time to blow off steam. Whether that would be possible in the coming days was yet to be seen.

Then, at seemingly the same moment, his three

companions answered their phones and simultaneously excused themselves from the room, all making the same muffled promise: "I'll be right back."

Will blinked and turned his head. It wasn't often he found himself in this position, standing alone in the middle of a silent, empty room. He looked around at the various doors through which Caroline, Bobby, and Larry had all left, then he arched his back and rubbed his neck. A moment later, the doors burst open again as all three returned, dragging the din of business along with them.

Caroline was carrying his duffle bag and a packet of papers. Will nodded goodbye to Larry and Bobby, who were still on their cells phones, and followed his assistant out of the room and down a long, dark corridor.

"Like I was saying," Caroline explained, "your flight leaves in an hour and a half, so you have to leave now."

"Car-" Will started.

"You have enough clothes for a week, but brace yourself, because unless you supplement your wardrobe, you're probably gonna need to do some laundry."

"Caroline-"

"I packed all your usual outfits. Hopefully things won't be too-"

"Caroline," he said

"What, Will?"

"Thank you. Now go, enjoy your vacation."

They stopped at a doorway at the end of the corridor. Caroline put her hands on Will's shoulders and looked him in the eyes.

"How are you doing?" she asked.

"I'm doing fine. I'm doing well."

She studied Will's face, looking for his tells, then held his gaze a moment longer, waiting for him to let his guard down.

"Have fun, Will. You have to. It's your family, and after all, it *is Saint Tropez.*"

Will just smiled and nodded.

Caroline gave him a kiss on the cheek, and pushed the door open to reveal a sea of camera flashes. Waves of voices crashed in on them from outside the arena's loading area.

"Once more with style," Caroline called over the cheering as she gave Will a gentle shove out into the chaos.

Will fumbled through the crowd of people, smiling, blinking in the glare of the flashes, and hoping to hell he seemed relaxed, that he didn't betray the tinge of panic that bloomed in his bloodstream on the rare occasions he found himself thus surrounded. He was met halfway by his driver and a bodyguard, who took the duffle bag from him and plowed ahead, leading the way through the throngs of people, clearing a path to the car. The sounds of camera shutters and questions were coming at him from all sides, and Will did his best to speak and nod as though he could hear what it was any of them were saying.

Then the back door to the limo opened before him, and he ducked inside. The driver walked around to the driver's side as his bodyguard closed the door and headed back towards the arena. Will looked out through the tinted windows as the people outside screamed and waved. The car pulled away, and he leaned back in his seat, watching the crowd and the camera flashes slide out of view.

—

He must have fallen asleep, for the next thing he knew, they were at the airport, and the driver was opening the door for him.

"Here we are, Mr. Baker. JFK."

Will lifted his head and smiled in sleepy confusion.

"Thank you."

He stepped out onto the curb and stood on the empty sidewalk, breathing in the humid summer air. It was after midnight, and the airport was uncharacteristically quiet.

The driver pulled Will's duffle from the trunk and handed it to him.

"Have a safe trip, sir."

"Hold on a second," Will said as he dug through his pockets in search of a tip.

The driver held up his hand as he headed back to the car. "Don't worry about it. Already covered."

Thank God.

As usual, he had no cash on him.

Will made his way through the desolate atmosphere of the late night airport. He got his boarding pass and dropped his duffel bag off at the check-in area, then passed through security, and headed down the seemingly abandoned concourse. He was just passing a newsstand when something caught his eye. He stopped and stared at the cover of *People* magazine. The headline read: *"Who is Fiona seeing now?!"*

The large letters were superimposed over a grainy photo of Will walking hand in hand with an attractive woman in sunglasses. They were separated by a jagged, torn-paper effect that ripped down the middle of the cover. Will stared at the image for a moment, then walked away.

As soon as he arrived at the gate, a flight attendant, no doubt recognizing him, if not *waiting* for his arrival after scanning the passenger list, immediately ushered Will onto the plane, past a smattering of fellow passengers seated in the waiting area.

A few moments later, he was seated alone in the empty first class cabin, sipping scotch from a crystal glass and staring out the window at the workers loading baggage and fueling the plane. With any luck, he'd be able to unwind and get a few hours of sleep on the flight overseas. The ice clinked in his glass as he raised his arm for a refill.

Saint Tropez

There wasn't a cloud in the sky. It was early enough that the sun was just filtering up over the trees, casting the swimming area in a warm pink glow, the light more like sun*set* than sun*rise*. Jen Cadwell, 30-years-old and athletically attractive, descended the terra cotta steps, set her towel on the nearest chaise, and padded around the edge of the pool, looking up at the sky, then down at the crystal blue water. The air was cool. She ran her hands up the backs of her legs and over her toned stomach to warm her skin. She knew from experience that the pool was colder than it looked, which was why she had to pace around it for a moment, rubbing her hands over the goose bumps on her arms, warming up physically and mentally before she took the plunge.

She walked to the deep end of the pool, looked down into the rippling water, then tensed her legs and dove in, barely making a splash as she slipped beneath the surface. Her arms and legs cut through the water, propelling her body forward as she sliced through the chill. She swam back and forth, five laps, then stopped at the side of the pool, resting her arms on the edge as she looked across the lawn at the main house. She turned to the deep end and gazed up at the apartment over the pool house.

He'd be arriving this afternoon. It had been ten long years since they'd spoken, though it seemed he was still everywhere she looked. Which, she guessed he kind of *was*. Funny the way things worked.

Jen's eyes gently drifted away from the pool house. She leaned her head back into the water to wet her dark hair and draw it together down the middle of her back. Then she pulled herself up and out of the water in one smooth motion, and walked up the steps to the lawn, where James Baker sat in a chaise looking over the pool area, a newspaper resting on his knee. He was on his Blackberry, like usual, only this time he was talking business, instead of hunching over the tiny gadget, mashing away at the keys with his thick fingers as he fired off emails. Jen watched him for a moment. James was a solidly built guy, handsome in a former college football star kind of way, but as his portfolio expanded, he was starting to show a bit of the signature swelling that so many of his Wall Street brethren inevitably took on around the middle. He'd fought it off better than most, but too many days spent at desks, on flights, and at business lunches, inevitably caught up with all but the best of them. It seemed the thirties were for making the money, while the forties were for getting back into shape and trying to escape the bloat of success. Going by those markers, James was about five years away from hiring a personal trainer.

Jen leaned down and wrapped her wet arms around him from behind. He recoiled, sitting up straight and covering the phone's mouthpiece.

"Jesus that's cold!"

Jen just looked back at him with wide-open eyes and a seductive smirk. James stared at her, then he started to turn back to the phone. He stopped and whispered to her.

"Just gimme a minute. I'm on the phone to New York here."

"Oh, *New York*. What an unexpected change of pace."

James ignored the mockery and returned to his call.

Jen furrowed her brow in mild irritation before grabbing her towel and heading toward the house. She passed Nekos Vlahakis who was heading out to the pool, towel and newspaper in hand. Nekos was James' uncle and another Wall Street vet. He was in his late 60s, well fed, and clearly enjoying his retirement, though Jen knew he still liked to keep up on the market as much as possible. Whether he'd admit it or not, James strove to emulate his uncle as much as possible, and if anyone could warrant a response by interrupting James' call, it was Nekos.

Jen stopped at the patio door and watched the older man sit down in a chaise alongside his nephew.

"How's the market doing?" Nekos whispered.

James waved his hand and hunched over a little.

"Just tell me how it's doing," Nekos asked again

James gave him a thumbs up and Nekos nodded his head. He had just leaned back in his chair and lifted the newspaper when his mother in law, Karen O'Connor, a sprightly 81-year-old, who was, as always, dressed casually but impeccably in slacks and a blouse, came walking toward him, a plate of pastries held before her, and his wife Anne – Karen's oldest daughter – following close behind.

"Oh, come on, Nekos," Karen started. "It's bad enough none of the men here can go ten minutes without checking the market, but you're *retired*. Enjoy it. Anne, would you tell your husband to relax?"

"I don't have the breath," Anne said as she walked past them and headed down the steps to the water, where she stood with her hands on her hips. Like her mother, Anne was almost unusually thin, and while this morning she was dressed for a swim, the majority of the time she was dressed to the nines in simple but chic designer outfits, not a hair or accessory ever out of place.

Nekos reached over and snatched a croissant from the plate. He immediately took a large bite from the pastry and shooed them away with the remaining half.

Karen set the plate on the table and shouted over to her Grandson. "James! I'm putting out some food."

James nodded to her and she headed back to the house.

Flakes of the first croissant still clinging to his lips, Nekos lowered his paper slowly, following Anne as she walked along the edge of the pool, studying the undulating surface. Confident that his wife wasn't watching him, he reached over and selected a chocolate croissant from the plate of pastries.

Anne's head snapped in his direction.

"Nekos, *no!* No more pastries!"

Karen walked back into the kitchen, passing Jen, who was leaning against the kitchen cabinet, observing the proceedings. Karen liked her grandson's girlfriend. She'd liked her since the very first time she'd met her. That must have been, what, seventeen or eighteen years ago now? Amazing how time flew by, and boy did it ever have a sense of humor. She'd never have expected this girl to return to the family loop, at least, not under *these* circumstances, but who knew, things didn't often go according to plan or expectations, and this visit would undoubtedly prove to be no different.

Karen poured a cup of coffee and studied her husband, George, who was sitting at the kitchen table, slicing up ingredients for that night's meal as he talked to their daughter Lucy. He somehow looked all of his 81-years, and yet... younger. Seeing him speaking with their 57-year-old daughter was a bit eye opening however, a clear reminder of how long they'd been together, and why they'd planned this entire trip in the first place.

One of their granddaughters, Peri, who at 36 was the youngest from their middle daughter's first marriage, was standing at the edge of the room, grazing on food and flipping through a fashion magazine. Stylish, but curiously indifferent to outside input on her appearance or demeanor, Peri was often found floating on the outskirts of conversations, throwing in observations about the parties mentioned, and voicing her amusement with throaty laughs of approval, mostly when her sisters were discussing a particularly odious mutual acquaintance. However, in family discussions, primarily those involving Lucy's kids, Karen noticed her granddaughter was frequently less than interested in prolonging the conversation.

"Lucy, what time does my grandson arrive?" Karen asked.

"Will's flight gets in at seven thirty, Mom."

"So, he'll be here by noon!"

"Probably earlier than that, assuming he can get a cab right away."

Peri's head shot up. She'd been leaning against the counter, licking butter from a table fork, but stopped short at the discussion of the morning's timetable.

"We don't have to wait around for him to get here though, do we, Pops?" She asked in her uniquely raspy voice. "We're supposed to go to the market this morning."

George looked irritated. "Relax, Peri. You won't have to wait for him."

Peri rested her hand on her chin, still looking put out. She raised her eyebrows as her sisters, Tracie and Maureen, walked into the room. At 38, Tracie was just a couple of years older than Peri, and though Maureen was Tracie's senior by more than three years, it was clearly Tracie who called the shots. She stopped outside the doorway, looking in the hall mirror as she straightened her Jackie-O glasses and brushed her black hair behind her ears.

"Who do we have to wait for?" Tracie called around the corner.

"Your cousin Will," George answered. "And nobody has to wait for him. The guy will probably just want to get here and go to sleep. He just finished a tour. I'm sure he's exhausted."

"Yeah," Maureen said as she leaned into the fridge and pulled out a finger full of whipped cream. "I hear it's grueling work going around the country singing for money."

Lucy looked at her father, who just rolled his eyes.

"It's not like you girls have ever had to-"

"*George,*" Karen said, cutting her husband off.

George looked at his wife, shaking his head as the three

sisters picked up their purses and headed for the door.

"*Anyway*, we're out of here," Peri said.

Maureen licked another scoop of whipped cream from her finger before following Tracie and Peri out of the room. "If you see our husbands, tell them we'll meet them at the beach," she said as she disappeared around the corner.

There was a moment of silence after the girls left the room. Karen, Lucy, and George looked from one to the other. No one felt the need to say anything more. The acrimony between the cousins had long been an unsuccessfully-dissected topic of discussion. Jen crossed the room, letting out a resigned sigh that said it all. She refilled her coffee cup and headed back out to the pool. Before this week, she'd had a decade long break from this family and its tensions, but the memories had come rushing back to her the minute she and James had touched down in Nice and rendezvoused with Tracie and her husband before making the drive down to Saint Tropez. Even years later, with her relationship to the family pivoted, her flag was still firmly planted on the Baker side of the equation.

Karen watched Jen through the window as she headed back to the pool.

"Does Will know about the two lovebirds? He's okay being here with them?"

Lucy stood and joined her mother by the window, watching as James walked over to Jen, his body language apologetic as he slipped his Blackberry into his pocket and shrugged his shoulders.

"Well, he knows about them, but I don't know how he feels

about it. He and James haven't exactly been close the last few years."

"Was it the girl?"

"That might have been a part of it, but they'd been growing apart long before that."

* * *

Will was jolted awake as the plane touched down on the runway.

He sat up and looked around the cabin as a flight attendant's voice bleated through the speakers overhead. The voice rattled off a brief schpiel in several different languages before switching over to English and welcoming them to Nice. Will slid the window shade up and squinted into the bright light outside as he watched the sparkling blue waters of the Mediterranean lapping against the tumbled stones where the runway disappeared into the water. In the distance he could see miles of beaches, with the tall buildings of Nice and Antibes set back a short distance from the water. The airplane taxid down the runway as he leaned back in his seat, rubbing his eyes, still exhausted from the trip overseas, and not nearly caught up on the sleep deficit that came with a months-long cross country tour.

You just need to stay awake a little longer, he told himself as he gathered his things at the gate and sleepily made his way his way through the airport.

The line through customs moved quickly, and he was soon standing in the baggage claim area, staring bleary eyed at the fresh stamp in his passport as he waited for his duffel to circle around the conveyor belt.

He scanned the waiting crowd, curious to see if he knew anyone, or as was more often the case, if anyone there knew *him*. If this were New York or L.A. he'd already have been swamped by now, but it seemed his fame had not yet stretched across the Atlantic to quite the same degree it had in the states. He hoped it would stay that way, at least for the time being. Not that he took the attention for granted, he just found it hard to speak coherently when his weary senses were overwhelmed by crowds of unexpected strangers. He was always afraid he was somehow being rude as he tried to get his eyes to focus on each person who swooped in on him from the periphery.

At last his bag came around the bend. He picked it up and headed for the exit, slipping on a pair of dark glasses as the double doors parted before him and he walked out under the overhang. A short distance down the sidewalk he came upon a young man in his early twenties who was leaning against a black Mercedes in the taxi area.

Will hesitated. His French was less than superb, or rather, it was non-existent. The best he could do was identify snails on a menu, and, he liked to think, correctly pronounce "croissant."

"Bonjour," the driver said.

"Bonjour," Will stammered. Believing broken English might make it seem as though he spoke just a touch of French, he continued, "Uh... Saint Tropez?"

The driver nodded. "Yeah, I can take you to Saint Tropez."

"Great." Will handed the kid his bag.

A moment later they were speeding down the highway, the driver whistling along to the radio as Will's head lolled back and forth atop his shoulders in the backseat.

The driver glanced at him in the rearview mirror. "Did you fly in from New York?"

Will sort of half-smiled as he glanced at the speedometer, hoping the kid would pay closer attention to the road.

"Yeah, I did. How did you know that?"

"This time of year, everyone flying into the airport is either British or American."

"So this is the big vacation time then?"

"Oh yes," the driver said. "When the weather is beautiful, everybody comes to the South of France. Lots of people. Lots of stars. Just like yourself."

Will looked up, bemused, as the driver nodded back at him.

"Is that right?" Will said. "Lots of stars...just like myself." He shook his head and smiled to himself.

So much for anonymity.

He turned and watched as the sundrenched countryside sailed by the window.

* * *

Will must have drifted off again, for the next thing he knew, the car was pulling through a pair of open gates and driving down a white, gravel-covered drive. The pea-sized stones shifted rhythmically between the tires, pinging off the bottom of the car. Funny how that one sound, so distinct, yet so universal, could signal a person's arrival at a luxurious getaway, no matter where in the world that might be. For some people, champagne corks were the sound of money, but as far as Will was concerned, gravel driveways were the truest audible sign of wealth. Renting this place must have set his grandparents back a fortune.

The driver parked the car and walked around to open Will's door. Will climbed out and stood to the side, sorting through a handful of cash as the guy grabbed his duffel from the back. When he came back around, Will traded him the cash for his luggage. The driver thanked him with a nod and headed back to the car.

"Enjoy your stay in Saint Tropez, monsieur."

"Merci," Will said awkwardly as the car began backing out of the drive.

Will turned, stretching and yawning as he moved, till he was looking at the house. It was picture postcard South of France perfect. An old, two story villa, with stucco exterior, blue shutters on every door and window, and thick, old grapevines circling up and around a wrought iron framework that stretched over the front patio. Birds called from a bank of trees to the right as Will trudged down the gravel walkway, passing between two rows of thick, fragrant lavender plants. The smell of the purple spikes filled his nostrils as he approached the massive front door. He knocked on the heavy wooden door and waited. No answer. After a moment's hesitation, Will tested the lock, pressing the handle down and pushing the door inward, cautiously.

"Hello?"

He leaned his head in.

"Anybody home?"

Nothing.

Will waited a moment longer, then stepped inside. He took off his sunglasses in the dim light and found himself standing on a red tile floor, in the middle of a white hallway. Beach shoes were lined up neatly on the floor against one wall. A dimly lit corridor extended to the left of the foyer. Warm daylight shone in from a hallway to the right. Shopping bags and purses were resting on a chair beside a hall table, where an enormous mirror caught his reflection. Catching a glimpse of the heavy bags under his eyes, Will hurried past the mirror, passing a doorway that led into the kitchen, and continuing on through the house till he was standing in the living room. Here too, the floor was covered with baked red tile. Massive, rough-hewn wooden beams stretched overhead, supporting the room's cathedral ceiling. Two long couches, and an assortment of oversized furnishings seemed to reach up towards the rafters above in an effort to fill the space. Will let out an appreciative whistle, then stepped back and headed into the kitchen.

The aroma of that morning's coffee still hung in the air. A platter of cheeses, each loosely wrapped in wax paper, rested on a windowsill next to the sink. A note with his name scrawled across the top sat atop a table in the middle of the room, held in place by a plate of pastries. Will picked up the note and selected a Danish, taking a bite as he unfolded the paper. He scanned the words quickly, immediately recognizing his grandfather's handwriting.

Will, you have the apartment above the pool house.
Everything is unlocked.
-Pops

He took the note with him as he cut through the living room and out the backdoor, slipping his shades back on as he crossed the threshold. A long table stretched from one end of the back patio to the other. This too was covered by a wrought iron overhang, where old growth grapevines clasped the metal framework overhead and swooped down over the dining area. A lush lawn, surrounded on both sides by small, well-manicured fruit trees, stretched from the house, across the backyard, and down to the *just*-visible pool area. He could see the water glimmering in the late-morning sunlight. Will slipped off his shoes and walked barefoot across the lawn, savoring the feel of the chilled, damp grass on his tired feet. He looked around him as he walked. This part of the yard was just as beautiful as the rest of the property. The grass led to a series of steps topped with terra cotta tiles that extended down and eventually surrounded the walkway around the pool. Overlooking the pool was a beautiful stucco building, with a gently curved staircase that ascended to a small apartment on the second floor.

Will stopped at the edge of the pool and stepped down onto the first stair in the shallow end. He stood there for a moment, savoring the cold water as the chill radiated up his body, cooling his system. Then he climbed out and continued on, leaving behind a trail of wet footprints that led across the walkway and up the stairs to the apartment.

Sunshine filled the room, filtering in through the shuttered windows, crisscrossing the bed, and reflecting yellow light off the walls around him. Will set his guitar bag on an armchair by the door, tossed his duffel in a corner, and walked over to the windows, where he threw open the shutters and stepped out onto a balcony overlooking the shimmering pool below. He felt the urge to head back down and dive into the water, but jetlag was catching up with him. Mr. Rock Star was hitting his limit. He could feel the weight of his eyelids drooping heavily behind his sunglasses. If he were to go for a swim, he'd probably lose consciousness and drift to the bottom like a rolling stone.

He turned around sleepily and headed back inside. This had to be the nicest, most secluded room in the place. Why had they given it to *him*? Before he could give it another moment's thought, the bed began calling to him. He slowly removed his shades, stumbled across the room, and fell backwards onto the sun-seared cotton sheets. He was asleep before his head had even hit the pillow.

* * *

When Will again opened his eyes, the light in the room had softened to a calming pink glow. He stared up through the rafters above him, to the room's cathedral ceiling, where a fan was slowly revolving overhead.

He could hear voices outside. The sounds of the cousins returning. It seemed they were approaching the pool area below his room.

Will heard his grandmother yelling to them from the house.

"You girls keep it down!" she said. "Will is probably sleeping."

There was muffled laughter, then the shuffling of feet and a snorteling guffaw that Will immediately recognized as belonging to Peri. A moment later, the *kablooshing* sound of someone doing a cannonball into the pool reverberated up to his room.

"Ahhhhhh!! It's *freezing*!" Peri shrieked.

"What did you grandmother *just* say to you?!" Pops' voice bellowed across the yard.

The laughter echoed even louder.

Will sat up with a groan and glanced at a clock by the side of the bed. It was just about 6:30. They'd probably be figuring out dinner plans shortly. He ought to say hello to everyone before the crowds skittered off to get ready.

He stood and walked out of his room, heading down the stairs. As expected, Peri was in the pool, treading water. She glanced at Will with a smirk, then nodded her head and slipped below the surface. Maureen was lying alongside the pool with her head in a copy of *Vanity Fair*. Will looked in her direction to say hello, but she didn't look up.

This was nothing new. For some inexplicable reason, there had been tensions between him and his three older cousins from as far back as he could remember. They either thought he was a hopeless country bumpkin, or they had a beef to pick with him over an issue they'd never bothered to bring to his attention. Things had only grown worse over the years, as lifestyles and politics, their wealth and his fame, seemed to accelerate the proliferation of resentments and perceived slights. He'd been struggling to find a way to maneuver this minefield of family dynamics for decades. Now he just tried to let everything roll off his back, but he had the sinking feeling that he'd inevitably reach the point where a sharp comment or a cheap shot would slip from his lips. He hoped he'd matured enough by now to keep that from happening, but suspected he couldn't be good the entire stay.

Whether Peri's cannonball wake-up call had been deliberate, he could only guess. The thing was, he really couldn't have cared less. Not yet anyway.

Will was just heading across the lawn towards the house when he saw his youngest cousin, Nekos and Anne's daughter Sara, running out of the house to meet him. At 21, she was nine years his junior, and one of his favorite relatives. As kids at Christmas and Thanksgiving they'd always hung out in her father's den, watching old movies. When they got older they'd sat on the back patio at her parents' place in New York, smoking cigarettes and sneaking wine as they looked out over Central Park and joked about the cousins. Will hadn't seen her in over a year now.

"Will! You're here!" Sara shouted as she ran over and gave him a hug.

"Hey, I was hoping I'd get to see my favorite cousin!"

Sara looked toward the pool. "Do I have competition?"

"I see they're here on their own. Where are their parents?" Will asked.

"Last I heard they were in Africa. Hunting lions or something."

Will wasn't sure if that was a joke or an accurate report.

His Aunt and Uncle were another anomaly in the family. While he was seen as the outcast rocker from Portland, the cousins' mother and father had suddenly up and moved from Long Island to a ranch in Montana five years before. Ever since then, they'd either spent their weekends stalking animals on their own property, or venturing off on globe trotting adventures, always making sure they bagged as many animals as possible in the process. Whenever he called his mother, he got a report that Harold and Esther were off on safari again. That they should go from a New York way of life to a Hemingway fantasy camp pilgrimage didn't surprise him entirely, and truth be told, he was somewhat amused by the bewildered state it left their three daughters in. When your parents are wearing leather pants that they tanned themselves, it's sort of hard to grab their attention with your latest Pucci top.

"How's everything going?" Will asked.

"Good. This place is a blast."

"That's what I've heard," he said with a nod. "You getting into enough trouble?"

"I could stand to get into some more."

"We'll have to do something about that. Maybe you can take me out and show me the hot spots."

"Now that you're here we'll be able to get *into* the hotspots," she replied.

Will's eyes darted toward Peri and Maureen. "How have they been treating you?"

"Oh, you know. They have their favorites. No sense trying to change 'em."

"Isn't that the truth," he said as the two of them ducked into the kitchen.

Lucy, Pops, and Anne were all sitting at the table. His grandmother was wandering around the kitchen, wiping down the counters with a paper towel.

"Well, look what the cat dragged in!" Pops said as soon he saw him enter. "Those girls woke you up, didn't they?"

Will shrugged and leaned forward to shake his grandfather's hand. "Hey, Pops."

Lucy hopped up and hurried around the table to give Will a hug. "It's so good to see you," she said. "How was your flight?"

"Good to see you too, Mom." He gave his mother a long hug. "The flight was okay. I can't complain."

Will winked at Sara as the questions started coming at him faster now.

"Any trouble finding the house?" Pop asked.

His grandmother and Anne walked over and hugged him as well.

"Now that you're here, relax," Karen said. "This is all our treat, everything but personal vices is on us. Sound good?"

"That means this isn't a free trip for Will at all, Grandma," Sara interjected. "All he *has* are vices."

"Funny," Will replied.

Lucy looked at her son with a smirk. "Will, vices? Never."

"You guys are a riot, really." Then he looked over his grandfather's shoulder and saw Tracie coming around the corner from one of the back bedrooms. "Hey Tracie."

"Oh, hey, Will," she said quickly.

"Where are the guys?" he asked her. He had yet to see either Tracie or Maureen's husbands.

"I think they went out for a run or something."

"The boys have been running every day," his grandmother replied as Tracie headed out the door. "I feel like we barely see them."

"Huh," Will said. "They planning some sort of escape?"

Sara stared at him, a smile twinkling in her eyes.

"And where's the rest of the crowd?" Will asked.

"Your uncle took James and Jennifer to a gallery near the port," Lucy said.

"A gallery?" That didn't sound like something his brother would do at all. "Was that Jen's idea?"

"Nekos is trying to turn James on to a local painter he started collecting a few years ago," Anne said. "He purchases a painting from his shop every time we come to Saint Tropez now."

"I never knew James had a thing for art," Will said as he looked at his mother.

Lucy just shrugged.

The room was quiet for a moment, then Pops broke the silence.

"Well, we're going out for dinner tonight. We've been alternating between meals at home and different places around the area."

"Sounds good," Will said as the crowd began to dissipate.

Anne headed for the door first. "I better head up and start getting ready before Nekos gets back and hogs the shower."

"I might as well get started myself," Lucy said as she stood, putting a hand on her son's back to steady herself. "Glad you could make it, kiddo." She gave his shoulder a squeeze as she walked away.

Sara walked over to the fridge and pulled out a green bottle of beer as Will's mother disappeared around the corner. "You want one?" she asked as she held out a Hoegaarden.

Will took it and twisted off the cap.

Sara opened another, and leaned against the counter as she took a nice, long sip. She exhaled loudly, giving Will a knowing smile.

"What?" he asked.

"Nervous?"

"No," he replied, trying to act clueless. "About what?"

"I'd be nervous is all."

Will took a swig of beer. "Get outta here."

"You *are* nervous," she said. "When was the last time you saw either of them?"

"It's been a while."

Sara hesitated, letting his answer hang in the silence. A bird whipper-whooled in the distance.

"Ever seen them together?"

He shook his head as he pulled a pack of smokes from his back pocket, tapped one out, and stepped outside. Sara followed him to the back patio, where he flicked open a Zippo and lit the cigarette.

"When was the last time you saw *her?*" she asked.

Will exhaled a cloud of smoke. "You ever stop asking questions?"

"Not if I can help it," she said with a laugh as she headed

back inside.

Will stood alone, watching the swirls of smoke dissipating around him in the pink evening light.

* * *

Will's favorite times on the road often took place at twilight, just before an evening gig, when the lighting and sound had been worked out, the crowds were gathering outside, and the band and crew could take a breather and relax, drink a beer or two, and just *hang*. He didn't get to do that as much during winter stops since most of the venues were indoors, where he couldn't take advantage of the fresh air, couldn't savor front row seats to some of the world's most beautiful natural music venues, like Red Rocks in Colorado, and The Gorge in Washington State. Something about this most recent tour, being free of a bad relationship and really on his own for the first time in ages, had reminded him of summer nights in a way he hadn't felt in ten, maybe fifteen years. He was happy to see that here on the Mediterranean, the summer nights crept in slowly, leaving an easy hour-long period between dusk and nightfall, in which the clouds pulsed with pink, the birds rustled in the trees overhead, and the stars began pushing through the surface of the lavender sky.

He padded down the steps from his pool house bedroom, savoring the smell of the sea as it wafted in from the harbor, and really loving the way his linen pants and shirt felt in the night air. The shower and shave had been refreshing, but the pants, hell, they were in a class by themselves! Linen, now that was a fabric he didn't wear much stateside. It was the fabric of destiny! Hell, these were the fucking *pants* of destiny. Damn were they ever comfortable. Comfort. That was what he was gonna need tonight if he planned to get through the evening's proceedings without incident.

He wasn't all that worried about how it would play out, he just dreaded the pauses between words, the awkward moments that he knew were coming, when he'd finally have to face the bizarre reality that his high school girlfriend, perhaps the one real love of his life, was dating none other than his older brother.

Will circled the pool, his hands in his pockets, checking to be sure he'd remembered his cigarettes and lighter. Drinking would be highly called for tonight, but cigarettes would be an absolute necessity. Reassured that lighter and flammable vices were on hand, he leaned down and dipped his fingers below the surface of the pool, letting the water drift up and over his wrists, just as Pops had taught him to do as a kid when he needed to cool off. He pictured the water chilling the blood below the surface of the skin, imagined the bloodstream rippling through his system and flooding his heart, the bracing temperature pulling the muscle taught. A cold heart and smoke in his lungs, just the ticket for-

"*Will?*"

He pulled his hand from the water, caught off guard. Despite his determination, he'd been unprepared for the sound of a voice he hadn't heard in a decade. He turned, looking over his shoulder to see Jen Cadwell walking toward him. She was wearing a light summer dress and looked almost exactly the same as the last time he'd seen her, only somehow, better.

"Hey."

"Hi there, " she said as she brushed a lock of hair behind one ear.

He walked over and gave her an awkward, rushed hug.

"Hi," he tried again. "It's good to see you."

And it was.

That was the worst part.

"What time did you get in?" she asked.

He watched her eyes, noting the tiny fold of skins just below the lower lids. They hadn't changed. The rest of her face had shifted, ever so slightly, like the surface had thinned, enhancing the delicate structure of her face. Her hair was lighter, but her lips were the same, and...

"I got here this afternoon."

He pulled the pack of cigarettes from his pocket and tapped one out into his fingers without thinking.

Jen nodded toward the smokes.

"You have an extra one of those?"

Will glanced down. "Oh yeah. Of course."

He handed her the cigarette and instinctively flicked his lighter open for her. She leaned the tip into the flame, then drew back and took a long drag as he took out another smoke for himself.

Without warning, she locked her gaze on him through the haze of smoke.

"I was wondering if you'd actually make it this time."

"I wanted to be there at Christmas, but things got hectic."

Jen nodded. "I completely understand."

And he knew she understood the real reasons.

"So how have you been, Will?"

"You know, I've been better, but I've sure as hell been-"

He was interrupted mid-sentence as his older brother approached. Will hadn't seen him in at least three years, and even in that short time, his brother had aged substantially.

James was playing with his tie, fiddling with the knot. "Hun, I can't seem to get this thing right." He looked up, realizing for the first time to whom Jen was talking. "Oh, hey, Will. How have you been?"

Will laughed, realizing he was still answering the same question, only posed a split second later by someone else.

"Oh, you know-"

Only then he was once *again* interrupted, this time by Nekos, who stepped onto the patio, booming out, "*Will!* You made it kid!"

"Hi, Nekos," Will replied, thankful for the interruption.

Nekos strolled across the lawn as Will climbed the steps and met him halfway. His uncle slapped him on the back and gave him a hearty handshake.

"How was the tour? I wanna hear all about-"

Yet now it was Nekos' turn to be interrupted. He bristled as a car horn blared out from the front of the house.

Peri could be heard shouting in the distance, "*The buses are leaving!*"

Nekos set his hand on Will's shoulder and shot him a look awash with irritation. "Those girls are driving me crazy."

Will shrugged in sympathy. He was afraid he'd share his

uncle's fatigue soon enough.

Will and Nekos rounded the corner of the house only to find Tracie standing between two mini vans that sat parked in the gravel drive. She leaned in through the first car's driver-side window and held down the horn. A low, sustained honk again moaned from under the hood.

"Hey, give us a break! You see us. You know we're coming," Nekos exclaimed, his words dropping with exasperation.

Tracie's husband, Arthur, a handsome man about three years his wife's senior, sat behind the wheel. He quickly nudged his wife's arm away from the horn in embarrassment and received an icy glare in return. Undeterred, or desensitized to her wrath, he leaned out the window.

"Sorry about that guys." He said to them before looking up at his wife. "Honey, I'm pretty sure we can wait just a bit longer for everybody to-"

Tracie cut him off as she raised a hand to her mouth, bullhorn style, and ramped up the orders. "Lets go people, buses are pulling out!"

Nekos again looked at Will, his eyebrows arched. "Boy am I looking forward to that first glass of wine tonight."

Will watched the scene unfold. If past experience was any indication, when one of the girls was on the warpath, it was best to let them have at it till they wore themselves out.

Jen and James emerged from the backyard and sidled up alongside Will and Nekos. The four of them watched Tracy and Arthur fighting over the car horn.

"This typical?" Will asked his brother.

"Pretty much," James said with a nod. "Sometimes they hit

their husbands with their purses. That's always fun."

Nekos headed for the van Arthur *wasn't* driving, where his own wife was waiting alongside Karen and Lucy, who were already seated. Will reluctantly made his way to Arthur's van. Knowing the way his extended family operated, he was already viewing this as the "kids" car, since growing up just about everyone in it had been seated together at the little table at Thanksgiving. The family dynamics had been just about the same back then, too.

Jen and James stood in the middle of the drive as Jen straightened the collar of his shirt.

The honking resumed.

A few seconds later, Sara came running out of the house, quickly scanned the occupants of each vehicle, and jumped in next to Will.

"Did you miss them or *what*?" she asked over the blaring horn.

"Are we running late or something?" Will whispered back.

"Of course not, hesitation and unoccupied moments breed introspection, which must be avoided at all costs. But whatever you do, don't brush off the impatience. They have no qualms about leaving a man behind."

"That's so... charming."

"That's family, my friend. That's family."

Tracie leaned on the horn again, sending out a fresh series of blasts as more of the family made their way out of the house.

Pops came strolling down the front walk, twirling a set of keys on his finger. "Tracie, knock that shit off," he barked, and the horn went silent.

Satisfied with James' shirt, Jen turned and watched the stragglers approaching.

Pops leaned down and surveyed the cars, counting the number of seats. "As usual, the kids are with Arthur," he said. "Adults with me."

James followed behind Pops, his hand resting on the small of Jen's back as he opened the door for her.

Will's jaw dropped as he watched the two of them climb into his grandfather's car. A line had just been drawn in the proverbial sand, and he'd been left in the playpen.

"That's right," Sara said, seeing Will's stunned expression. "We're in the kiddie car."

"Who else is in here?"

"Just you wait and see," she answered ominously.

The rest of the family was still trickling out of the house as Tracie glanced at her watch. Will couldn't help but notice the way her shoulders relaxed as her sisters, Maureen and Peri, emerged from a side door and headed for the kids van.

"Lets get going people," Tracie said again, but now the words lacked the same inexplicable sense of urgency.

"Maureen, where's your husband?" Arthur asked.

"How should I know?" Maureen muttered. "He'll catch up."

Tracie walked around, climbed into the front passenger seat, and slammed the door closed behind her. Will winced at the force of the sound.

"We need to get going," Tracie commanded.

Arthur reluctantly put the van in gear and started turning

around in the drive. He looked back at the house in the rear view mirror as he slowly stepped on the gas. Suddenly, Maureen's husband, Clayton, appeared in the reflection, emerging from the front door with a cocktail glass in his hand.

Maureen let out an annoyed sigh and leaned out the window, shouting to him over the sounds of kicked-up gravel as they peeled out. "You can go in the *other* car!"

Clayton shrugged his shoulders, took another sip of his drink, and walked over to the adult car as the kids van took off down the road without him. The corner of his mouth hooked up in an impish, almost imperceptible smile.

Jen had employed tunnel vision as best she could as she and James passed the others en route to the van. The brief interlude with Will had been easier than she'd expected. Easier, that was, until the moment she got close enough to get a whiff of his aftershave – it was the same brand as a decade earlier, the same he'd *always* worn, something with chamomile and a sort of "hippy" essence that she'd never been able to pin down. Feeling just the *tiniest* creepers of anxiety tickling the base of her neck, she'd hoped the cigarette smoke would dampen the smell and knock her olfactory flashbacks to the side, but damned if that sweet, sharp smell of fresh-lit tobacco hadn't completed the package and pulled her back through the years.

James had provided a welcome distraction, and Nekos' usual booming interruption had given her an opening to step back, collect her thoughts, and redirect her attention to the brother she was with *now*.

It was funny, but aside from one or two little mannerisms, a way of brushing something from their eyes, or the way they held their mouths as they paused between thoughts, there was very little about the two siblings that would ever call the other to mind. That made it easier. And she cared for James, she really did, so the less distraction, the fewer tipoffs to make her doubt the roots of her own affections, the better.

Yet, as she stood in the driveway tinkering with his collar and trying to keep her eyes from darting, even briefly, in any direction but James', she couldn't help but find her fingers worrying a spot along her lover's jawline, the place where he so frequently seemed to miss a few stray whiskers with his razor. She didn't know if it was the result of the slight thickening around his neck, or just a general obliviousness, but it happened with some degree of consistency now, and meaningless as it was, she couldn't help but admit that it bothered her at the moment.

As the van up ahead rounded a corner, she caught the briefest profile glimpse of Will. He was seated in the backseat next to Sara. No surprise there. Jen's eyes scanned his jawline and the tight flesh at his neck. Then the setting sun glimmered off the side window and he vanished in a flash of light, just as the car disappeared around the next bend.

So far as she could remember, Will had never missed a spot when he shaved. And though she liked the way he so often let his scruff grow out, she'd always loved giving him a long, soft kiss on his neck after he'd just shaved.

This might be a tougher vacation than she had expected.

The vineyard was beautiful. The old vines stretched out into the distance under the ever-darkening sky. The last glimmers of daylight scorched the horizon, even as the stars floated to the surface. The smell of honeysuckle wafted past, waltzing in the air, along with the singed aroma of a wood-fired oven.

Will's family: the three cousins, two of their husbands, and his aunt, uncle, mother, and grandparents, stood around the back patio behind the restaurant, visiting and drinking as they waited for their table. Music emanated softly from hidden speakers. Will stood on the corner of the stone platform, sipping a deliciously crisp glass of rosé as he took in the sunset. A tiny yellow dog was sitting under a nearby table looking up at him with pleading eyes. Will leaned down and scratched him behind his ears.

Clayton walked up behind Will and tapped him on the back. "Good to see you, Will. I've been trying to get a hold of you for a couple of weeks."

Will scratched the dog under his chin, then stood up and took another sip of his wine. He looked in Clayton's direction as he swallowed.

"Have you? I'm sorry, things have been hectic the last few months."

"So I've read," Clayton replied.

He was no doubt referencing the magazine and gossip sheets plastered with Will's face and details of the big breakup. What nobody realized yet was that today's gossip was yesterday's history. Will had been half-heartedly extricating himself from that fiasco for what felt like ages. It was just that details were only now filtering into the media about what had gone down.

"Listen," Clayton continued. "I want to talk to you about a couple of your accounts, get your thoughts on some changes."

"You don't even have to ask. Everything you've done so far has been great."

"Well I'm glad you're happy, but I'd still like to be sure you're aware of the thinking behind my decisions. It could wind up saving you a lot of money."

Clayton leaned against the stone wall that surrounded the patio as he settled in to talk business, but as soon as his wife glanced over and saw him conversing with her cousin, she stepped away from her sisters and walked toward them. Her eyebrows lowered as she caught snippets of the conversation.

"You've already saved me money, and you've *made* me more cash than I know what to do with."

"That's why I'm here my friend."

Maureen cut in, sharply, "Clayton, Will has accounts with you?"

Clayton looked at his wife in confusion.

"I've had Will's accounts for years now. You know-"

"And you have the time for that?" she interrupted.

The look of dismay on Clayton's face grew as he put his arm around her shoulder and led her away from the conversation. "What are you talking about, Maureen?" He whispered in a raspy hiss as he led her a short distance away

"Your cousin is one of my biggest clients."

Will pretended he was oblivious to the whispered conversation. If his cousins didn't want to have anything to do with him, that was fine, but he was more than happy to let their husbands put their investment acumen to work for his portfolio. Clayton was a good guy. He lived in a different world, one Will was never too eager to visit, but the guy had made him some very good money. Will also knew that having him as a client probably helped Clayton keep his wife in the lifestyle she preferred. That, in and of itself, was the sort of rich irony that Will couldn't help but enjoy.

Before Maureen could respond to her husband's comments, the host came over and led the family to a long outdoor table that stretched across the back of the restaurant's patio. The views of the vineyards were even more breathtaking from this point of view. The family reached the table and everyone started taking their seats. The waiter returned a moment later and began filling their water glasses. Will took a sip and sized up his location. He was caddy corner from the triumvirate of his cousins, who, as usual, were busy discussing their four favorite things: Travel, fashion, gossip, and New York City.

His mother and the other "adults" at Will's end of the table were wrapped up in the menu.

Anne flagged down the waiter and requested four bottles of rosé. After the waiter had left, Will had to ask about them.

"So, what is it about rosé in the South of France?"

His aunt looked at him like he'd just crawled out of the woodwork. "When you're in Provence in the summer, in

Saint Tropez *especially,* you *only* drink rosé. It's like water. You don't even know it has alcohol in it."

"Excuse me," Will's mother Lucy cut in, "but the hangover I had this morning *definitely* reminded me that there is alcohol in the rosé."

"Okay, let me correct that," Anne laughed. "The majority of folks don't feel any ill effects. My sister down there is the lone exception."

Will held up the quarter glass of rosé that remained in his glass, swirling it gently as he peered through the rippling layers. It glowed a warm pink in the candlelight. He brought it to his lips and downed the rest of the glass.

Nekos was looking over the menu.

"Anything look good?" Anne asked.

He tilted his head back and forth in a so-so motion. "I just need something to eat or I'm gonna have a headache. Can't afford to wait for the kids to stop talking and start picking out their meals."

"Aren't the majority of *'the kids'* approaching or well into their forties?" Will asked.

Nekos looked up and swatted his question away with the flick of a wrist.

Will laughed.

All the while, the volume at the far end of the table was growing. Peri, who Will was beginning to think resembled an early-80s Kirstie Alley, was recounting the list of demands she'd handed down on her most recent first-date.

"So, I told him if he wanted anything to happen, he'd better get down to the dealership and start pricing the Jag he'd need to buy me if he *ever* expected me to carry and raise his spawn."

"Oh my God," Maureen interjected. "Speaking of cars, did you hear about Sarah Oliver's accident?"

Tracie's head shot up. "*Talk* about a tragedy. And she'd just had that nose job last year! Such a waste."

"I'm telling you, don't buy an American car!" Peri added.

Arthur raised his hand slightly, like a student waiting to be called on in class. "Well, she *was* under the influence, and going 95 in a 20, wasn't she?"

"That's beside the point," Tracie snapped.

Maureen took a long sip of wine as she watched the conversation ping pong among the participants. "Didn't they adopt a baby?"

Tracie reached across the table and swiped a knife full of butter. "Yeah, Korean-"

"Oh. Couldn't they..." Maureen let her sentence drift off, seemingly completing it with a wiggle of her hand into the air.

"I guess that's what you get..." Peri said with a resigned nod.

"Dead?!" Clayton exclaimed. "I hope you're blaming the drunk driving, and not the decision to-"

Tracie once more shushed her husband.

Will leaned over and whispered in Sara's ear, "Do you have any idea who these people are that they're talking about?"

"I haven't got a clue. If I did, I'm sure I would be appalled."

A clinking sound emanated from the end of the table as Pops tapped a fork against the side of his wine glass. The group slowly quieted down.

"Excuse me people," their grandfather began. "I just wanted to take a moment to welcome the latest addition to our little gathering."

He swept his hand in Will's direction as the cousins rolled their eyes at one another.

"He's been busy on tour, and he's very much in demand with folks in the record business, so I think we should all be honored that Will could make it here to spend three weeks with his grandmother and I, helping us celebrate our 60th wedding anniversary."

The group murmured their real or reluctant concurrence and clinked their glasses together. They were still sipping their wine as Nekos rose to his feet and lifted his glass.

"I'd just like to add something else, something I think is really important to express at a time like this." He turned his head, looking off to the side as he took a deep breath. "Oh *shit...*"

Will blinked. Then he mouthed the words to Sara: *Oh shit?*

Sara pointed to a table in the far corner, where a severe couple in their 70s sat holding wine glasses in mirror image poses. They were glaring at the family's table with matching expressions of pure hatred.

Peri let out a high-pitched guffaw, only to be silenced by a series of shushes from the "adult" end of the table. She covered her mouth and snorted as she looked from Tracie to Maureen.

"That German couple has been at every restaurant we've gone to for the last few days," Sara said. "For some reason they just sit and glare at us the entire time."

Will studied them from the corner of his eye. "Jesus. What's that all about?"

"We can't figure it out."

"Think it could be Peri's cackle?" he whispered.

Sara stifled a laugh. "I've wondered the same thing!"

Nekos looked around quickly, then sat back down in his chair.

"Anyway, just glad everyone can be here," he muttered sheepishly. "I'll say more later."

An anxious din filled the air as everyone reached for their wine glass or looked for the bread.

Will scanned the group. The cousins weren't paying attention, but Jen looked up just as his eyes passed over her face. They studied each other for a second, then Will shrugged his shoulders to feign confusion.

Jen raised her eyebrows as if to say 'Who knows?'

Arthur, who up until then had been silent, took a deep breath and broke the tension. "So, Tracie and Maureen have a couple of really big projects coming up when we get back."

"Oh yeah!" James replied. "I've been meaning to talk to you two about that. Jen and I are gonna be looking at places soon, and I thought you might be able to help us with one when we get settled."

"Help us with what?" Jen asked him.

"Maureen and Tracie have started a lifestyle consulting agency," Arthur replied.

Jen looked at him for a beat. "A what?"

"They're lifestyle consultants," James said.

"And what is that?" Jen asked as she sipped her wine.

"We do clarifications for clients," Maureen said matter-of-factly. "We tell them what they need to get if they want to stay in fashion. We help them set up their clothes, their homes, we pick out their cars-"

Tracie cut in. "Whatever someone needs help with, we step in and take it over for them."

"So, you're... counselors?" Jen asked.

Tracie seemed annoyed. "No. We tell people what they should like."

"Then you're dictators?" Jen laughed. "You're kidding, right? I don't get it."

Tracie and Maurren looked at her with straight faces.

Jen realized they were dead serious. "So, you're telling me you guys tell people who don't *know* what they like, *what to like?*"

"Exactly," Maureen replied.

Jen looked at James. "And why do *we* need this?"

"Everyone needs this," James began. "I was just reading about it in the Times. It's the next big thing."

"It really is the key to success," Maureen began. "You cannot do business in New York if you aren't up on what's current. You need the right home, the right clothes, the rights books, you need to talk about the right shows."

"Who decides what's right?" Jen asked.

"We do," the two sisters replied in unison, as they exchanged flummoxed glances.

Jen held a hand to her cheek, trying to resist the compulsion to speak. Finally, she couldn't hold back any longer. "Yeah... but see, I *have* style. I *have* taste. If we get an apartment together. I think it should say something about both of us."

Tracie dabbed at the corners of her mouth with a napkin. Her lips were pulled tight, as if concealing fangs. "Well then, that's fine. It will say something about you, and something about what Maureen and I feel James would like to say."

Jen wasn't going to let this one drop. "But, isn't that saying he's too shallow to express something for himself?"

James rubbed his belly. "Hey now, I like to think I've got *some* depth," he interjected, but his attempt at humor landed with a thud.

Tracie folded her napkin and set it on the table. "You know, Jen, maybe you shouldn't talk about something you don't understand."

Jen was blindsided, and briefly stammered for words as she tried to maintain her composure. Finally, she replied, "I understand all right. This is just a way you two can get paid for doing what you've always done, snipe about strangers' clothes and houses behind their backs. Well I'm sorry, but I don't need or want your help."

"Maybe you don't," Maureen commented. "But James does. You like that outfit he's wearing?"

"What does that have to do with anything?" Jen asked.

Tracie reached for the rosé and refilled her glass, "We helped him pick that out. We redid his whole wardrobe last fall."

"Look," Jen began. "We aren't going to need this *service* of yours anymore."

"And how will you know you're getting the hottest things?"

"I don't care if my home has all the hottest things, that's not the point."

The girls looked back at Jen blankly.

Maureen blinked and turned her head five degrees to James. "We'll talk," she told him. Having mentally erased Jen from the picture, she then stage whispered to Peri, "Some people just don't know what's good for them."

Caught off guard, having failed to diffuse the situation, James sat dead in the middle of things, avoiding eye contact with anyone at the table.

All Jen could do was look at Will pleadingly. He gently bobbed his head in sympathy.

Nothing had changed.

* * *

As if following the directive of some telepathic memo to avoid socializing, the family scattered the moment they returned home. There would be no late-night powwows in the kitchen that evening over further glasses of rosé.

James considered going for a swim, but seeing as the markets would be closing within the hour back in the city, he decided it would be better to check his email and make sure nothing had gone wrong during the trading day.

Will made no mention of his own potential itinerary before he wandered out to the back patio. To his surprise, Jen lagged behind in the kitchen for a moment, before eventually following him out back and sitting in the shadows on a nearby bench. Will leaned against the wall a few feet away as he looked out across the moonlit lawn. Frogs were croaking softly under the plants out in the darkness. The air had cooled and taken on a dewy, damp freshness in the nighttime breeze. A car horn sounded in the distance, the rumble of an engine zipped past the end of the driveway at the entrance to the property. He could hear the water circulating in the pool as the pumps came on. The sounds of the car faded into the distance as he and Jen were left alone in the calm atmosphere of a midsummer evening.

Eventually, Will pulled out a cigarette and lit it with a flick of his lighter. The glow illuminated his face, and cast just enough light that he could see Jen's expression as she looked up at him expectantly. How many times had he seen that look on her face in his lifetime? He walked over, handed her the cigarette, and sat beside her. She took a long drag and exhaled a cloud of smoke.

"They're killing me."

"The smokes?"

"Your *cousins*."

"Oh, yeah, they tend to do that to people." He reached for the cigarette, took a drag, and handed it back to her. "They're like a tag team of overtightened windup toys."

Jen laughed.

"Didn't I make that comparison the Christmas I spent with you on Long Island?"

"Probably. You know I've never been above lifting a good line."

"You realize I have to deal with them on a daily basis now,

don't you?"

Will rubbed his temple for a moment.

"I guess that's what you get for picking the older brother."

He caught a flicker of red light as it glinted off Jen's eyes. "Will, let's not go there."

"Where?"

"You know."

"I'm just saying-"

"Seriously, just stop," she said.

"You know I hate being told that."

Jen took another quick drag.

Will could tell she was getting agitated. He probably wouldn't be getting that cigarette back.

"When your brother and I got together, we, you and me, had been history for ten years."

"Nine."

She paused – doing the math – and shook her head when the numbers failed to support her case.

"The point is, I didn't choose one over the other."

"But in the long haul, you *did* end up with him," Will replied as he reached for the smoke, but Jen pulled her hand back just as it was within his reach. He watched her expression to see if she'd done it on purpose. "And before that, *you* left *me*," he continued. "Why was that again?" Now he was the one getting a bit annoyed.

But if he was annoyed, Jen was flat out angry.

"*What?*" she countered.

"Why was it that you left me again?"

She finished the rest of the cigarette and mashed out the

butt.

"We were looking for different things, Will. I wanted to grow up and be an adult. You wanted to hang out in bars and play music with your buddies."

He sighed softly as he tried to relocate the central thread of the conversation. A fight was really the last thing he wanted, but old reflexes had led him back to a wound he thought he'd left far in the past.

"So, how's that adult thing working out for you?" he asked.

She hesitated, looking down at her feet as she brought her hands under her thighs.

"It... *sucks*. I hate it."

Will turned to say something, he opened his mouth and was about to speak, but Jen stood before he could gather his thoughts.

"Have a good night, Will," Jen said as she got up and walked inside.

Will was left sitting alone in the shadows. After a moment, he shook another smoke from the pack of cigarettes, fired it up, and sat watching the light from the pool as it glimmered off the water and rippled over the leaves overhead.

* * *

Jen stood in her nightgown, washing her face in the bathroom sink. She glanced in the mirror as she saw James walking up behind her. He wrapped his arms around her and kissed her on the neck.

"What was all that tension with Tracie and Maureen?" he asked.

She turned around, resting her hands on his shoulders. "I'd really rather not talk about it."

"You don't think that we should?"

Jen looked into his eyes, holding his gaze for a moment before she leaned in and gave him a long, gentle kiss, and led him into the bedroom.

"No," she said. "We shouldn't."

~

Will sat alone in the moonlit darkness of his room, strumming his guitar softly. The blue glow from the pool rippled across the ceiling and walls around him.

He was thinking of Jen's second year of college, when he'd followed her to Syracuse and they'd moved in together. She was a full-time student while he'd gotten a gig working on home renovation projects with a local contractor. It wasn't good pay, but it had covered his half of the rent and paid his bar tabs when he sat in with his musician buddies at shows and tippled a few glasses of scotch. Eventually, the sporadic gigs, as well as the rotating roster of band members, had given way to a consistent line-up and a couple of standing appearances at some of the local hot spots. The band had been a little rough at the beginning, but even from the start, Will knew they had unique chemistry, something he'd never felt with any of the other groups he'd been involved with. He could still remember the night of the first practice, when he came home and sat at the kitchen table afterwards, peeling the damp label from a bottle of Honey Brown as he shared his hope with Jen that maybe, just *maybe*, this group had something unique going for it. He couldn't remember if her face had registered optimism or a trace of doubt.

Soon after that, he wrote a few songs, and they lined up some more gigs – mostly at bars that didn't card, which was good, since Will was just twenty, and their bass player, Steve, was only midway through high school. As word of mouth spread beyond Syracuse, they started to travel a bit. The road had been slow going at first, a night here, another gig two weeks later. Then they made some tapes, and some of the folks in the audience started to record a few of their shows and pass the bootlegs around, until slowly but surely they formed a listening base, and the offers started flowing in.

Unfortunately, just before the music and the group started to gel, Jen had decided she'd had enough. To be honest, Will really couldn't blame her. They're been together for five years, almost all of them in high school. They kept things going long distance the first year of college, then he'd joined her in Syracuse for the second, but between her school and friends, and Will's increasing commitment to the band, their lives had been changing dramatically, and the altered pieces no longer fit together in quite the same way. They tried to make it work, but at some point, he couldn't remember how, or why, or even when it had finally happened, they'd eventually broken it off.

The breakup had been her idea. He knew that much.

Jen dove into school.

Will hit the road full time.

And the rest was history.

But whenever he wrapped a recording session, or finished

a tour, Will always found himself alone someplace, thinking about Jen. He couldn't help himself.

Now here he was, playing his guitar, while the love of his life was back in his orbit, just across the yard in fact, and horror of horrors, she was with his brother.

~

They lay in the dim light.

One of their longer interludes. But Jen wasn't sure how she felt about it.

She kept her head pressed against James' side until she felt him reaching for his Blackberry on the nightstand.

"Please don't," she said. But he didn't hear her.

She stood and walked into the bathroom, where she turned on the hot water in the shower and waited for the room to fill with steam. Then she stepped under the stream of water, savoring the feeling as it beaded off her face.

Too many memories were coming back to her.

Another time, and another life.

She stood under the showerhead for a long while, closing her eyes as the hot water coursed down her body. Eventually, she turned off the water and stood in the stillness, feeling the water dripping from her nose and chin, imagining the trails of beads as they trickled through her hair, over the small of her back, and down the length of her legs. She listened to the water as it circled the drain. Finally, there was only silence. The bathroom windows were open, letting in the sounds of the night. A draft of cool air whispered over her skin. She opened her eyes, wrapped herself in a towel, and walked out into the bedroom, where she found James passed out on the bed, his little Blackberry bobbing up and down on his chest. Jen watched him for a moment to be sure he was asleep, then she crossed the room and pulled open a drawer in the lower half of an antique armoire. She moved James' shirts aside, and felt underneath for the ring case she had stumbled across just a few days earlier. Her fingers brushed against the crushed velvet and she pulled it out. Another glance over her shoulder, then she flipped open the lid, and stared down at the diamond as it shimmered in the light.

She thought she should be feeling excitement, or nerves, or *something* now, but just one sensation settled in her chest. It was the same thing she had felt days earlier when she'd first flipped that lid open. Confusion.

Jen turned at the sounds of crunching gravel outside. She slipped the ring back into the drawer and walked over to the window, where she looked down at the courtyard and saw Will walking down the dark driveway, disappearing into the night.

~

It was a short walk into town. Just a turn around the bend, a leisurely walk down a tree-covered dirt road, and he was out on the main drag, where cars passed him, and the late night club-goers were making their way to Saint Tropez's well-known hotspots. Will passed under the sign for Byblos, that oh so famous Page Six stalwart, but he wasn't in the mood to dive into the usual celebrity scene. Maybe if he'd seen Nicholson or Jagger lumbering up the long, ivy-covered staircase he might have felt differently, but he really wasn't in the mood to chase women, or party with that crowd. Not tonight. He needed to clear his mind, namely by muddying the waters. In short, he was in the mood to drink.

So he walked past Byblos, and past the downtown square where the market took place twice a week. About a block further, tucked into a largely unadorned stucco building, he came upon two double doors that opened into an elaborate hotel lobby. Past the lobby he could make out the pale blue glow of a swimming pool in the middle of an open courtyard. Past that he could see the bar.

A doorman stood guard - the place was undoubtedly funny about non-guests or the less than elite stopping by to rubberneck. But whether by fame, or attitude, Will had learned long ago to behave as he pleased, act like he owned the place, and do whatever he damn well wanted. When you acted that way, VIP or not, people tended to step out of your way.

He strolled inside, feeling the doorman watching him from the corner of his eye, but no one said a word. There were no hands on his shoulder, no pseudo offers of "help." They left him alone. He continued on through the lobby and out to the cocktail lounge in the courtyard, where the smells of cigarette smoke, burning candles, and spicy food lingered in the air, collectively stoking Will's thirst for a beverage.

Two hours later, he was staring at the bottom of another glass, enjoying the tingle in his teeth, trying to discern if there was any feeling left in his legs.

There was just a smidge.

He'd need another drink.

He slid the thick crystal glass across the polished cherry bar top, where it clinked against an empty comrade. He'd been ordering them in pairs, each time making a joke about Noah or ants marching, chuckling aloud at his humor, until the bartender's transparent irritation threatened to cut him off. After that, he'd ordered each round with two raised fingers, and tossed them back quietly, despite his good humor.

Will noticed the service had slowed considerably in the last hour. The wait staff was probably trying to ease the flow of booze through his bloodstream. What was this, *America?* Why couldn't they just let him get smashed?

Then again, he probably needed to put on the brakes. He was at that glorious drunken tipping point between reverie and despair, but one sip too many could send him over the edge at any moment. Plus, a hangover in the hot sun would really suck tomorrow. He sat there for a moment imagining the motion of waves undulating before him.

A pistachio shell hit his glass.

Then another.

What the fuck?

He swung to the left.

Nothin'.

Then he swung to the right. Two little hotties in tube tops were standing a few seats down. They giggled to each other and muttered something under their breath. They were Americans. And *damn* if they weren't cute. A blond and a brunette. Always a complementary pairing.

'This might go someplace,' Will thought to himself, then wondered if even his internal monologue was slurring out into the real world.

He smacked his lips contemplatively.

"Hi," the blond said softly.

"Well hello," Will said as mellifluously as possible given his condition.

"We know who you are," the brunette whispered as she leaned forward.

"Oh you *do*, do you?" Will whispered back. "And who *are* I? I mean - who *am* you two ladies?"

The girls giggled and moved closer. Now they were standing alongside him.

"We have a question for you," the blond replied. "Ever been with two girls at the same time?"

He smiled from ear to ear. "Is that a question, or an offer?"

"Would you like to find out?" the brunette replied as she pulled on his arm.

Will shrugged his shoulders in compliance.

They giggled some more.

Will staggered to his feet and started to follow them, but his foot got caught on the leg of his stool, and he crashed to the floor before he realize what was happening. The room grew quiet as the people at the surrounding tables turned in his direction.

Stunned, but still game, Will looked up at the two women as a trickle of blood burbled from his nose and ran down over his front teeth. "You got a room here girls," he slurred.

"Dude," the dark-haired girl said. "You're more fucked up

than we thought.

They exchanged looks.

"I think you might be out of luck tonight," the blond added.

They helped him to his feet, but their flirtatious intonations had vanished.

Will sat on his stool, his head hangdog, as he watched the girls walk away. The bartender walked up to him and Will turned to him instinctively.

"A double," he said as he held up three fingers.

The bartender waved his hand through the air in a slicing motion. He was cut off.

Will looked around the room, unsurprised, and not entirely disappointed, then he staggered to his feet, rummaged through his pockets for a wad of cash that he then set on the bar, and stumbled out through the hotel lobby and off into the night.

* * *

Jen had been doing her best to get a run in every morning. Some days she made it, some days she slept in, but she was starting to notice a distinct pattern: The days she managed to get up early and head out before the rest of the family was awake, usually came after someone or something had managed to get her sufficiently upset the night before.

This morning, as she ran through town, passing the usual assortment of vacationers picking up pastries at the boulangerie, she realized she was mentally rehashing the latest run-in with James' cousins. Even as the aromas of fresh-baked baguettes, steaming espresso, and almond paste stirred her hunger, she was all too aware of the way her mind was working now. She wasn't thinking of breakfast, and she wasn't remembering *just* last night, her thoughts were rolling back even further, back to her high school and college days, when she and Will had been together. Even in those days she'd struggled to find her comfort zone around the cousins, and since back then she had assumed she and Will would be together for the long haul, she'd tried to find a way to thicken her skin for the inevitable holiday gatherings with his significantly different relatives. She had to admit, when the two of them split up all those years ago, the tense interactions with certain members of Will's family were one aspect of their relationship that she hadn't missed. Now here she was again, trying to find a way to fit in and sail unscathed through the inevitable familial tensions.

Thinking about the past made her think about Will – how he was now, and how he'd been back then. He'd changed a lot over the years, but at the same time, he was still very much the guy she'd fallen in love with as a girl. At this stage, those remaining boyish qualities were immeasurably more appealing than they'd seemed when she was in college. In Syracuse he'd started to seem like an overgrown boy, not to mention an equal opportunity flirt. She didn't think he'd ever cheated on her though. Will Baker didn't fuck around on people, not if they meant something to him, he just didn't make much effort to let the people that *mattered* know how much they meant, and to her way of thinking back then, showing how important she was to him, meant he needed to act like an adult. Playing in a rock band and hanging out in bars seven days a week, that wasn't acting like an adult. Not in her book anyway.

Christ. It was embarrassing to think back to those days.

She was 21 when they called it quits, and when she recalled her reasons for the breakup, what she'd *valued* at that age, she might as well have been fifty.

Will was a musician and an artist. He'd *always* been those things. That was part of what drew her to him in the first place. Unfortunately, life, particularly in college, has a funny way of quietly twisting a person's mind in knots, 'til the things your parents value suddenly seem important to you as well. It's a scary day when you start pondering employment aspirations and career arcs, mortgages and retirement plans, a scarier day still when you realize you've bought into all that bullshit hook, line, and sinker. That's when a lot of people suddenly realize they've lost sight of the things in life they really want to be doing. The funniest part of it all is that as people eventually grow up and enter the death march of working life, far too many of them start reading about and *envying* the folks who somehow hung on to their childlike dreams and went after the lives they'd always dreamed of leading. Steve Spielberg was one those guys. Stephen King was another. And in Jen's life, Will Baker was the ultimate example of what a person could attain when they stuck to their passion and didn't, not even for a second, consider selling out and going for the safe career path.

Will had always done just as he pleased, and damned if he hadn't come out on the other end happier and more successful than anyone she knew. Including herself.

Now here she was, in a situation she'd never have predicted for herself, and all she could think about was the aching sense in the bottom of her stomach that she had made a terrible, terrible mistake. For the life of her, she couldn't seem to stop turning that faraway decision over and over in her mind.

Jen's mind snapped to attention as she headed into the long straightaway before the house. This was when she really liked to push it. She stared straight ahead as she pumped her arms and legs, pushing her body till her limbs began to feel numb.

Numb and alive.

Birds were chirping in the trees on either side of her as she raced past. Her hair was tied back in a ponytail, but the front still rippled in the wind as she ran.

The home stretch.

Push it!

She ran harder now, her arms and legs pumping, her head tipped back, eyes turned up to the sky.

A little further.

Just a little further.

Then she hit the end of the driveway and gradually slowed her pace as her shoes crunched over the fine pebbles. After a few yards she returned to a walking stride, her hands resting on her hips, gently massaging the bones beneath the skin and muscle. She walked the length of the drive and continued up the pathway toward the front of the house, stretching her arms and legs as she approached the main door. She listened for sounds from the kitchen, and felt her stomach tighten a little at the clinking sounds of dishes being pulled from the dishwasher.

The house was awake.

She entered through the front door, walking past the entrance to the dining room, and headed into the kitchen, where Arthur and Clayton sat at the table talking on their phones. Jen poured herself a cup of coffee, selected an almond croissant from a plate heaped with goodies, and headed upstairs. She was halfway up when a fleeting glimpse of the pool house caught her eye through the window on the landing.

Nekos passed her as he headed down from the second floor, en route to the pastry tray. "Good morning," he said.

Jen smiled absentmindedly, pulling her attention from the pool house. "Good morning," she murmured.

Nekos, oblivious to her distracted response, was already steaming into the kitchen. "How's the market?" He asked Arthur and Clayton the moment he caught sight of them.

Arthur lifted his hand and made a "so so" motion.

James came around the corner, immediately motioning to Arthur and Clayton's phones.

"Hey, can I borrow one of those? I need to check the Dow."

"James," Pops interrupted as he marched around the corner, dangling a set of car keys, "The market can wait. You are on vacation in the South of France! You should try to enjoy it!"

"I know, Pops," James conceded. "I'm trying."

"Trying or not, the adult van leaves in three minutes." Pops spun the keys on his finger as he walked out of the room and past the dining room table, where his granddaughters were all laughing about something they'd just read on Page Six on their phones.

"Girls," Pops bellowed. 'Buses are leaving."

Peri's eyebrows popped up in surprise.

~

Will lay on the floor.

He was growing increasingly aware of the harsh sunlight that glowed red through the lids over his closed eyes.

His mouth was gummy.

A car horn blared.

He smacked his lips.

Damn.

The sound reverberated inside his head.

Honnnk!

Stop... *honking...* you... *assholes...*

Ho-O-ooooooonk!

He opened his eyes. The sunlight was searing. His head was throbbing.

HoOOOooooooooooooonnnnnk!

Fuu-uuck!

Now he was getting mad.

He opened his eyes and stumbled to his feet in a pissed off little burst of energy.

The horn honked a fourth time and Will felt his blood pressure spike.

His head throbbed again. His skull seemed to be closing in on his brain.

What did he have to drink last night? Why did he *ever*

take to drinking in the first place?

The car engine revved outside, and Peri's voice called, "Bus is moving out! Last call!"

He heard the sounds of doors and shutters slamming closed at the main house as family members rushed to batten down the hatches and run to the vans before they were left behind.

Will looked down. He was shirtless, but he had apparently changed into his swim trunks the night before.

He had absolutely no idea how that had happened.

Sara's voice rang out from across the yard, "Hold the *van!* I'm *coming!!*"

Will looked around. He snagged a linen shirt from the back of the chair, grabbed a pair of sunglasses, slid his feet into his sandals, and headed on his way. His head lolled atop his shoulders like a sand-filled balloon as he descended the stairs.

Sara climbed into the van, her swimsuit, towel, and book were wrapped up in a ball like something Linus might have carried in *Peanuts*. She scowled at Peri, who was staring at her watch as she absentmindedly tugged on her earlobe.

Peri's eyes shot open suddenly. "Oh shit," she said to Arthur. "Hold on, I forgot an earring."

Peri leapt out of the van and ran back to the house as Sara looked on in disbelief.

Will stumbled around the corner, looking sick as a dog as he passed Peri, who was struggling to unlock the deadbolt on the main door. Her head spun in his direction as he walked by. Her crestfallen reaction confirmed his suspicion that she had been hoping he would miss his ride to the beach.

Will ignored her, instead turning his attention to the plate of leftover pastries that sat on the front patio table.

Peri smacked the door with the palm of her hand and the lock finally opened. She ran inside, the sounds of her flip-flops echoing as she angrily stomped her way up the tiled front staircase.

Will lowered his sunglasses as he studied the plate of breakfast goods. He selected a chocolate croissant, slipped it into his pocket, and headed on his way.

Peri came running out of the house a moment later, pulling the front door closed behind her as she fumbled with her earring. She hustled down the driveway to the van – where Will was just sliding the door closed – jumped into the passenger seat, and gave Arthur the nod. The van lurched forward with a roar. Sara looked sympathetically in Will's direction, but he had already fallen back to sleep, his head slumped against the headrest, his mouth hanging open.

The van took a winding route along the edge of town, working its way through the narrow side streets, until it intersected with the main road that headed out through the vineyards in the direction of the water.

Will opened his eyes cautiously as he took in the sun-drenched views of row after row of grapevines, then he shifted his hangover-heavy head, and peered through the windshield as Arthur slowed down at an intersection and took a left onto yet another side road. The van rounded the corner, and there before them was the Mediterranean. Clean and clear and impossibly blue, the crystalline water was highlighted by just the faintest of ripples moving across the surface.

The van cruised down the hill toward the water. About a block before the road terminated at a public beach, Arthur steered to the left, past a sign reading *le club 55*, and pulled to a stop in a dirt parking lot. Three tanned young men – one with long hair, the other two with close-cropped buzz cuts – all of them dressed in matching blue and white shirts – greeted them with smiles as Arthur climbed out of the vehicle. The first short-haired guy went over to the adult van up ahead, which had apparently arrived just a few minutes earlier, and took the keys from Nekos, who in turn handed him several folded bills and headed for the boardwalk to the beach.

The longhaired attendant came over to Arthur's side of the car with a *'Bonjour'* and took the keys from him as well.

The second attendant opened the passenger and sliding doors, looking up with a broad smile when he saw Will stepping out, just as he was taking a big bite of pastry.

"Ah, bonjour, Monsieur Baker! Welcome," the young man said in a thick French accent. "I didn't see your name on the list today."

"Thank you," Will said as he nodded hello and tried to swallow the mouthful of food. "I'm here with family, so I probably wasn't on the list."

"Ah, that would explain it!"

Will caught the cousins exchanging sidelong glances as the attendant went on to wish him a good stay in Saint Tropez.

"If there is anything you need, just ask," The attendant said.

Will brushed his flour-covered hands on the front of his shirt and shook the guy's hand.

"Thank you very much. I appreciate it," he replied.

The group from the kids van started walking down the boardwalk that ran around the bamboo-covered edge of the club's back dining area. Sara caught up to Will just as he slowed his pace to ensure he stayed a few yards behind the rest of the group.

"Have you been here before?" she asked.

"Never."

"Interesting," she said with a nod.

Will looked around at the tables and chairs tucked in among canvas sunshades and twisting, knotted tree branches. Sandy walkways wove their way among the tables, up to the place where an older man in his 60s, with wavy gray hair, white pants, and a white linen shirt, stood on a platform looking out over the dining area. The man's arms remained crossed as he watched the group pass by, but he raised his head when he saw Will, then raised one hand in greeting as if he too recognized him.

"I'd swear these people all know you," Sarah mused.

Will let the observation go without comment.

They probably did.

Several more people lifted their heads as the family

approached the beach. Will Sara, the cousins, and their assorted husbands, all caught up to Nekos. Pops and the other adults were standing at the beach attendant's desk talking to yet another young man, who confirmed their reservation, then grabbed a pile of beach mats and umbrellas and headed out across the beach. The family followed behind, with Will taking up the rear as they wound their way among a beach full of gray-haired men, playing children, and topless sunbathers. A few men stretched out on beach chairs nudged their female companions and motioned in Will's direction. The cousins fanned out away from him.

The attendant set a beach mat on the sand under a thatched beach shelter and tucked a smooth wooden back support behind the cushion. Nekos promptly draped his towel over the pad, dropped his sunscreen and book in the sand, and sat down in the shade. He looked up at Will, all smiles.

"What do you think, kiddo?"

"Fantastic," Will replied as he spread his towel out in the sun alongside him.

Nekos looked out across the water, turning his head in either direction to take in the scene. He breathed deeply and nodded his head in appreciation as two gorgeous women, their skin tanned a golden brown, wandered topless down the beach just a few yards away. The wind gently tousled their hair as Nekos slowly shook his head.

"France is a glorious country, isn't it?"

Nekos watched, entranced, as a beautiful young woman in her early twenties, dressed in a pair of white bikini bottoms, walked about ten feet in front of where he and Will were sitting. She looked in their direction cautiously, then stopped.

"Will?" she asked in an American accent.

Will looked up as Nekos' jaw dropped.

"Hey, how are you?" Will asked.

"I'm a lot better since I've seen you," she replied as her fingers twirled her hair absentmindedly. "You in town for a while?"

Nekos watched dumbfounded as the girl stepped forward and crouched down beside the thatched beach shelter.

"Yeah, I am."

"You should stop by Byblos. I'm there every night."

Will cracked a Cheshire cat crack grin. "Maybe I'll do that," he replied.

She flashed a mischievous, narrow-eyed look and stood up.

"Then maybe I'll see you there," she said with a smile as she turned and walked away.

Nekos savored her departure from the corner of his eye. "Who the hell was that?"

"Oh, just a girl I've hung out with on the road a few times."

"Hung out with on the road. Some rough life you're leading, Will. Some rough life."

* * *

The morning drifted by, with the various family members reading on the beach and sleeping in the shade. Occasionally, Karen and Pops would get up and go for a swim. James, Clayton, and Arthur bought British papers from a vendor who walked up and down the beach, then read them intently before they began checking in with their offices every thirty minutes. All the while, their wives took turns glaring at them over half-read fashion magazines.

"Scowl all you like," Arthur said, "but this is how we pay for Piping, ladies."

Jen didn't nag James. She just read her book and watched the people passing by. She looked over at Will a few times to see how he was doing, but he'd been out late the night before and was now passed out on the beach like a pickled platypus.

When the sweat on her brow and back reached critical mass and began beading on the surface of her skin, she set her book in the sand, stood and stretched, and headed down to the beach. The water was cold but refreshing as it lapped over her toes and up around her ankles. She waded in quickly, feeling her diaphragm contract as the water slipped up around her ribcage. Then she swam several quick laps back and forth, parallel to the shore, before she lay on her back in the water and floated contentedly.

Jen listened to the muted sounds of children's laughter as her ears slipped beneath the surface, and watched the people on the beach as they wandered in and out of view.

She felt like an alien around this crowd, like she wasn't ever truly welcome. She wondered if she'd always feel that way, or whether something had changed inside her, particularly in the last 24 hours. Even James seemed distant when they were surrounded by his family, like he was straddling two worlds, a rotund colossus attempting to exist in a benign no man's land. Everything between them was feeling awkward and forced. The only person she suspected might really know how she was feeling, who was probably feeling the exact same way, was someone she didn't entirely think she should be speaking with or thinking *of* at all. This was all feeling awkward and bizarre, like a kinked up version of a Shakespeare comedy.

She studied Will's sleeping form. What was running through his head at this moment, other than recalcitrant scotch bubbles? There was a time during high school and college when she could just about read his mind. Back then they'd spent every waking and sleeping moment together. She had been with this family many times before, and even then it had been a strange, strange dynamic. The adults had always been welcoming, it was just around the cousins that things seemed... strained. She and Will had *always* felt like outsiders around the group, and strangely, that had felt somehow *right*. But now here she was with Will's older brother, and he seemed to be seeking entry to the club. In fact, he already seemed to have one foot in the door. And somehow, that had left Jen feeling all the more isolated.

She closed her eyes for a moment and slipped below the water. The cold pulled her scalp and eyelids taught. She snapped her legs together and propelled herself back up above the water, where she dunked her head back to draw her hair together and down her spine, before trudging back to shore.

-

Jen rinsed off under the outdoor showers, dried herself with a towel, and walked over to the gift shop. She was looking through a spinner of sunglasses when she heard Peri talking to her sisters in the back corner of the shop.

"Oh God, this shirt is so cute."

"Let me see," Tracie replied.

Then Maureen's voice cut in "You should get that. Do they have any more?"

The sounds of furiously shuffled coat hangers filled the air.

"I don't see anything."

"*This* is cute!" Maureen exclaimed.

Jen looked over and saw Maureen's arm shoot up across the room, a beach top held in her fist.

"You should try that on," Peri said as the sisters made their way toward the back of the room near where Jen was standing.

Jen ducked back behind the spinner, trying to avoid them as they gathered in the corner. Their voices were louder now. Jen shuffled over to a rack of beach towels as two English women made their way past her to a rack of bathing suits behind the girls' new encampment.

"Did you see who showed up this morning?" The first woman asked.

Jen peered around the corner to sneak a look at Peri, Tracie, and Maureen, who had stopped in mid-conversation. Peri was holding up a shirt, a disgusted expression frozen on her face as she listened.

"No," the second woman answered. "Someone big?"

"Very." Then in a whisper she said, *"Will Baker."*

Her companion let out a little sigh. "Is he still here?"

Jen's mouth hooked in a little smile as Peri sneered to her sisters and lowered the shirt she was holding.

"I don't want this," she said.

"The stitching is for shit," Tracie concluded as her sister tossed the shirt on a table and the three of them walked out. Jen watched them go, her eyes twinkling with satisfaction.

-

The family sat clumped on shore, sizzling under the hot sun.

Now and then Nekos would lower his spy novel to survey the beach and take in some of the local "scenery."

Will looked around, still floating in a sun-drenched, hungover haze. He kept drifting off to sleep before waking with a start. Eventually, he awoke to the sound of his grandmother's voice.

"William, you are getting fried."

Will looked up at Karen's silhouette. The sun behind her had grown harsher.

"Am I?" he asked.

He dropped his head to the towel and looked sideways across the beach, noting the heat waves rippling over the sand stretching down to the water.

His grandmother crouched and handed him a bottle of sunscreen.

"Word is you've been having a hard time," she said matter of factly.

"Who told you that? This is the first break I've had in months. I'm having a great time."

Karen shook her head impatiently. "I'm not talking about the trip. Everybody damn well *better* be having a great time while they're here. I'm up on the cultural news, Will! I still go through the grocery checkout line. I can recognize my own grandson's face on the cover of *People* magazine." She paused dramatically. "Now, how are you doing after your split with that *Fiona* girl?"

"I'm doing all right. That Fiona girl and I weren't such a great thing." Will smiled. "How are things going with you and that George fella?"

Karen looked over at Pops. "They're going just fine. Can you believe I have known that man since *high school?*"

Will's eyes instinctively darted toward Jen.

Pops looked up and motioned for Karen to come over. She turned back to her grandson for a moment, as if debating what to say next. Then she reached out her hand, brushed the hair away from his forehead, and stood and walked away. She passed Sara, who walked past and collapsed in the sand next to Will.

"You feel like partying tonight?"

"Actually, yeah," Will replied, suddenly realizing his headache had eased. "I was thinking of going to Byblos later. You game?"

"Are you kidding? I've been wanting to go there since we got here."

"I'll call 'em from the house and have them put my name down. You have any friends you want to come with us?"

"Yeah. That'd be awesome!"

"I figure we can sneak out after dinner. Maybe I'll meet you and your friends down there."

* * *

The restaurant the second night was noticeably more formal than the vineyard had been. The family was spread out around a long table that stretched across one side of the room. To enter the establishment, they had taken a flight of stairs down from street level, where they found themselves at one of end of a massive dining area resembling a wine cellar or underground cavern. The feeling was intentionally amplified with the addition of roots that crawled down the walls and hung from the ceiling over the tables. There was a distinctly haughty way about the waiters, and the diners seated at each of the tables had a much more chic, particular manner about them.

It seemed everyone in the group had their own unique reaction to the atmosphere. Karen was all smiles as she placed a cloth napkin in her lap and looked around. The cousins glanced from side to side, scanning the room for notable diners.

Will was numb to the surroundings and more interested in the wine list. He reached across the table for a heavy leather binder with grapevines embossed on the cover, and briefly caught Jen's eyes as he did so. They exchanged glances, then each turned away.

Jen whispered to James, who was shifting in his seat uncomfortably.

"You're so fidgety tonight."

"Am I?"

"Yes," she said. You're driving me nuts."

James looked around the room. His eyes settled on a silver haired man in his sixties, who was leaning back in his chair, savoring a glass of wine as his 30-year-old dining companion looked on.

"I bet there are some nice portfolios in this room," James said.

Jen sighed. "Yeah, that was my first thought too."

George was seated on Jen's left. She could hear him whispering to Nekos as the two of them surveyed the room.

"Any sign of that couple?" George asked.

"I think we're in the clear," Nekos whispered back.

Will was still looking over the wine list when a young man carrying a camera suddenly emerged from around the corner. Will didn't see him at first, just noticed his shadow out of the corner of his eye, but when he looked up, he was face to face with a camera lens. The flash popped in sync with the sound of the camera shutter. When Will's vision cleared a moment later, he saw two waiters rushing across the room and grabbing the man by his elbows. A brief tussle ensued before a large kitchen worker in a stained apron came lumbering out of the back to assist in the photographer's removal.

"I'm very sorry about this Monsieur Baker," one of the waiters said as he grabbed a loaf of bread from the family's table and socked the cameraman in the face with it.

The blow was just enough to set the man off balance, and the cook and waiters were on top of him immediately, quickly pulling him away from the table and dragging him up the stairs at the opposite end of the restaurant.

The commotion drew the attention of the other diners, who turned silently and looked in Will's direction. The majority of them appeared miffed as to his identity, but a few of the women seemed to recognize him. Will nodded nonchalantly as one girl held up her phone and snapped a pic.

Then the manager was at their table, delivering a fresh loaf of bread as he turned to Will. "Monsieur Baker. I deeply apologize for the intrusion."

"It's really no big deal," Will replied, as he noted the irritated glares coming at him from the end of the table. "It's certainly not the first time that's happened," he added, just to watch Peri and company bristle.

The manager noted the wine list in Will's hand and motioned for him to lift it where he could see. "Nevertheless," he said in thickly accented English. "I would like to send you over two bottles of the wine of your choice, with our compliments."

Will looked up at him and begged off, "That *really* isn't necessary."

The manager nudged the list forward. "I'm afraid we insist."

"Well, if you insist," Will shrugged. "We'll take whichever one you'd suggest."

The manager ran his finger down the list. Nekos lifted his eyes as the manager's finger slid down the page and stopped at the bottom.

"I believe you'll enjoy this one very much sir."

Nekos eyebrows twitched above his eyes like dancing caterpillars.

Will just smiled.

"I'm sure that will do quite nicely," he nodded.

"Those are nine hundred dollar bottles of wine!" Nekos

whispered as the manager walked away.

Will shrugged his shoulders sheepishly. "What else could I do? Should be good."

"Should be *great*. I'm really starting to appreciate this lifestyle of yours, kid."

~

The night drifted on.

Wine arrived. Food arrived. Wine arrived again.

The complimentary bottles gave way to the inevitable rosé, which gave way to repeated orders of the light pink wine that flowed like water across Provence. Eventually, Will looked up and realized that seven empty bottles stood scattered across the table, and the conversation at the "kids' end" had grown noticeably louder and contentious. The usual suspects appeared to be dominating the discussion. At the moment, Tracie had the floor, and her voice rose to ensure she would not soon be pushed from her place of power atop the soapbox.

"So, apparently Harvey Weinstein threw an utter fit when he saw the proposal for the cover, and confronted the editor at Dan Buckley's birthday party."

Jen looked up, seeming a bit surprised. "He did?"

Tracie ignored her and plowed ahead with the conversation. "There was a huge to do. The two of them get into a shoving match, and Harvey ends up on his back in the middle of the museum's fountain."

Will watched Jen curiously as she again tried to break into the conversation.

"Excuse me," Jen said. "But where did you hear this story? I was at that party. That was last March. And that didn't happen at-"

Maureen set her glass of wine down and spun in Jen's direction. "Just because *you* didn't see it, doesn't mean it didn't happen."

Jen's face grew flush.

Will wasn't sure if the red in her cheeks was from too much rosé, or whether it was the result of pure irritation. He suspected a combination was at work.

"Excuse me, Maureen, but-"

Then Peri cut in, attempting to wrest control of the conversation in order to hand it back to her sister. "*Anyways.* Tracie, you were telling a story."

Tracie looked from the left to the right and cocked her head at an angle. "Well, apparently some people would rather I not tell this story without running it past them."

Will felt a flush of heat in his own face. Now *he* was starting to get pissed. He could feel a slight pulsing in his ears as Peri's words hung in the air.

Tracie continued, "I supposed I'll just pick up with that story later. Peri, you work over there. What have you heard about Tina Brown coming back?"

"What do you want to know?" Peri said, trying her best to sound uninterested.

"Is it true?"

"I think that's extremely unlikely!" Jen said.

Tracie tried to power through. *"Is it true?"*

Jen leaned back in her seat and glanced at James, who was

wrapped up in a market discussion with Arthur and seemed to be oblivious to the conversation. Jen looked at Will, but he was staring in his cousin's direction.

Peri was scratching at the top of her head as she spoke. "There have certainly been rumblings. But nothing is definite as of yet."

That's when Will laughed out loud. A deep guffaw erupted from his open mouth before he even realized what he was doing.

"Now wait a second. Wait one *second!*" Will blurted out. "Peri, humor me for a moment now. The last time I heard, what was your position at *The New Yorker?* Has it changed?"

"No," she said coldly. "It's the same."

"So then, you're still a customer service phone representative?"

Peri glowered at him, then nodded coldly.

Will looked at her and arched his eyebrow.

"Among other duties," she said.

"And now, Jen," he asked. "What's your position at *Electron Toast?*"

"I'm the managing editor," Jen responded.

The adults were starting to turn their heads towards the kids' end of the table.

Will lifted his hands, playfully imitating the motions of a scale. "Okay then. Customer service rep. Managing editor. Managing editor. Customer service rep... I'm *thinking* managing editor is probably the more connected position. Probably have a better scoop on the inside track. Wouldn't you think?"

Will turned to Tracie, feigning contemplation, but quickly cracked a broad smile. She was flinging visual daggers his way. He held her gaze a moment longer, then turned back to Jen.

"Now then, do you have any information on Tina Brown?"

Jen crossed her arms and locked eyes with him. "Tina's launching a new website with Will Bartleby. She's out," she said after a beat.

"Tina. Is. Out."

Peri took a deep breath. "Well that's not what we've been hearing."

"Hearing where," Will asked in breathless innocence. "On the phone board? In the staff break room?"

"Will, why do you have to be such an asshole?" Maureen hissed.

"Because those are the only people you girls respect," Will replied with a wolfish grin as he ripped into a dinner roll with relish.

* * *

"What the hell was that all about?!" James asked.

He was standing in the middle of their bedroom, shirt untucked, face red with irritation as Jen stood in the bathroom, removing her jewelry.

"What was *what* all about?"

"That, *outburst!* What's wrong with him."

Jen walked into the room, her hands pulled up to one ear, removing a diamond stud. "Are you talking about *Will?* He was defending me against your cutthroat cousins James. I appreciated it!"

Jen set her earrings on the bedside table, slid out of her dress, and returned to the bathroom.

"Cutthroat cousins?" James wondered aloud.

"Did you even *notice* what was going on tonight? They either shut me out or cut me down, every night. They're bullies."

"That's just-"

Jen stood in the doorway, her voice rising. "That's just what? That's just the way they are? James, you know I'm not making this up. They're sharks. You've said that yourself. They circle their territory and look for blood in the water."

"I think that's being a little dramatic. Don't you think you might be seeing things as being a bit more hostile than they really are?"

"Maybe so," Jen responded, a moment before she stepped out of the bathroom in a bathing suit. "But I wouldn't ever want to be the type of person who brushes that kind of thing off."

James watched her as she grabbed a towel and walked out of the room.

Will was just walking down the driveway when he heard footsteps padding across the back patio, heading down to the pool. He walked back to the corner of the house and glanced over the lush plant beds in the direction of the pool, where he saw Jen drape her towel over the back of a nearby chaise, then stand at the deep end, looking down into the sapphire blue water as it shimmered under the night sky. She was motionless for a moment, then her legs tensed, and she dove into the water. Will watched as she swam several sharp, quick laps back and forth across the pool. When she stopped at the shallow end, resting her arms on the terra cotta walkway, he turned and trudged off into the night, heading toward town.

~

Saint Tropez was jumping. Many of the revelers had clearly just driven down from the north for the weekend, and the more affluent vacationers had apparently decided it was time to cut loose. Will walked through town, passing crowds of partygoers dressed to the nines, along with older yacht dwellers who were strolling the side streets, clad in pink and turquoise linen shirts, many of them carrying miniature dogs in their arms. The occasional car horn blared in the distance. Music was thumping from several of the more trendy bars. Will made his way through the square to Byblos, where he ascended the long, gently-inclined staircase that ran beneath a thick canopy of ivy and flowers as it wound around the building to the pool and bars above.

He emerged at the top of the stairs, and looked around the upper deck. A few couples, the so called "beautiful people," were swimming in the pool, stopping in separate corners to kiss, and smile, and reach for the glasses of wine that waited for them poolside. Lights were aimed up at the colorful buildings that housed the hotel's luxurious rooms. In the back of his mind, Will couldn't help but wonder how many of the guests – the wealthy, the famous, the notable, and the notorious – were behind those walls, making love before coming down for the evening.

He lowered his gaze and looked in the direction of the covered bar, which sat under the meridian blue sky of stars. His eyes twinkled in the light. He was tired. A little down, but still ready to have a good time, especially when he caught sight of the two friends Sara had brought along.

Sara waved to him as he made his way through the crowd.

"Here he comes," Sara said to her friends.

Maura and Christie were classmates at Grimwood University back home. Maura was a brunette. Christie was a redhead, who seemed to be a magnet for men.

"Him?" Christie asked as she recognized Will. "*That's* your cousin."

"Yep."

"Do you know who that is?!" Maura chimed in.

"I know. Pretty cool, right?"

Will was still making his way toward them, a crooked, sort of sheepish smile on his face. Both of her friends looked to be the same age as Sara, and both were attractive, but his eyes locked on the red-haired girl, who had a little something extra going on. She was *striking*. Finally, he slipped into a calm pocket in the middle of the crowd and coasted to the table.

"Hello ladies," he said to the three of them.

"Hey," Sara replied. "Will, these are my friends from school. This is Maura-"

She put her hand on the dark haired girl's shoulder.

Will stepped forward and took Maura's hand. "Maura. Hello."

"And this is Christie."

"Hi there Christie," he said as he clasped the red-haired girl's hand and held it just a fraction of a second longer, running his fingers up to her wrist and looking her in the eyes. He glanced around the group.

"What's everybody drinking?"

"Rum and cokes," Sara answered.

Will motioned to a waitress as she slipped past.

"Three rum and cokes, and a glass of Dalwhinnie," he said. The waitress nodded and Will turned back to the table. "How long have you girls been here?

"Just an hour," Maura replied.

"You in town for long?"

"A couple of days," Christie said.

The waitress returned with their order, handing each of the girls identical drinks, and handing the Scotch to Will.

Sara laughed. "That was *fast*."

"Was it?" Will asked. He turned his attention to Christie. "Are you here with family or just by yourselves?"

The two friends exchanged looks.

"We're on our own, for now..." Maura said.

"So, you're here for pleasure I suppose."

"Yeah, I guess you might say that's the goal," Christie said.

Will winked. "That's the best one I can think of."

The girls laughed flirtatiously as Sara rolled her eyes.

"How long will you be in Saint Tropez?" Maura asked him.

"That's still up in the air."

Will glanced down at his drink, realizing they all had yet to take a sip. He held his glass aloft and the three girls joined him in a toast. "Ladies, to a great evening."

They clinked their glasses together as the music on the dance floor came thumping to life.

The first round went down fast.

The second even faster.

Before he knew it, Will was in the middle of the room, dancing with Maura while Sara and Christie laughed and danced with one another. Then he was with Christie, dancing close, whispering in her ear, feeling her body pressed against his. Smelling her hair, feeling her breath - hot and fresh on his neck. He pictured the music, felt it moving around them, and let alcohol and sound propel him around the floor.

Hours and hours, drink after drink later, the four of them left Byblos, wandering down the same long winding staircase Will had walked up alone. When they reached the bottom, they strolled down the sidewalk out of town, until they hit the long dirt and gravel road that led back to the family's rented house.

Christie was leaning against Will. She was giving off a certain vibe, one he knew all too well from his years on the road. When she started asking him about his own songs, and quizzing him on their meaning, he knew he was good to go. He played along, part of the routine, the game. It never got old, not with a girl like Christie.

"Sing that one song," she said as she ran a finger over his lips.

He murmured the words to one of his most well-known tunes. The bread and butter early work.

"Nope," Christie said with a giggle. "That's not the one.

He stopped singing. "That's not it?"

"It's more like that older one. It's kinda dirty."

"Ohh, I know the one you want," he said with a grin. "Why do you wanna hear *that* one?"

She fell against him, a little sloppy, but still bewitching. "I just do," she whispered.

"Why?" he whispered back.

She pressed her mouth against his ear. He heard her draw in a long, slow breath, before she suggestively replied, "Because it makes me want to do things that I probably shouldn't be doing."

Sara and Maura looked away, feigning disgust as Will cracked a broad smile.

"Well then, I better not sing that one..."

Christie put her arms around Will's neck. Her legs buckled and he stumbled under her weight as she laughed softly. They continued on down the tree-covered path until they arrived at the house. The windows were all dark, the family long since gone to bed. Even from the front yard they could see the rippling blue lights reflected from the pool's surface onto the branches that hung over the backyard. They walked the rest of the way down the driveway and up the path to the front door. Sara wrestled the key into the lock and let them in. Will walked through the darkened living room, stopping to stand in silhouette in front of the glass doors that looked out onto the backyard.

"Ladies," he said drunkenly. "We'll have to do this again some time."

"See you in the morning, Will," Sara said.

Will fumbled with the handles on the door as he unsuccessfully attempted to make his exit without turning his back on the girls. Finally, he got the door open, gave them one last sheepish smile, and stumbled off in the direction of the pool house.

Christie began to follow Sara and Maura upstairs, then stopped.

"I'll, uh, be right back," she whispered.

Maura and Sara exchanged knowing glances as Christie headed for the back door.

Will kicked his shoes off into the shadows and walked across the lawn in his bare feet. The grass was dewy on his skin. He took a cigarette from his pack of smokes, stuck it in his mouth, and fumbled through his pockets as he walked down the steps to the lighted swimming pool. He heard footsteps behind him and looked up to see Christie stopping at the top of the stairs.

"What are you looking for?" she asked seductively.

"I think I left my matches back at the bar."

She padded down the steps toward him. "You shouldn't play with fire, Will," she said as she moved closer.

Will looked her in the eyes as she wrapped her arms around his neck.

Christie reached up to his mouth, took the cigarette between her long, slender fingers, and flipped it into the pool. She pressed her chest against him.

Will set his hands on her waist as she roughly pushed him backwards. He caught his footing at the edge of the pool and gave her a funny, almost nervous look. She kissed him softly, then bit down on his lower lip. When she took another step forward, the two of them tumbled backwards into the pool. Christie let out a playful yell as she came back up to the surface and swam over to him. She wrapped her legs around him and stared into his eyes. They floated in the middle of the deep blue water, kissing passionately.

~

Jen lay awake, her eyes sparkling in the dim light that glimmered in through the bedroom windows. She listened to the sounds of splashing water out in the darkness, strained to catch the tone of a girl's gentle laughter, and waited for the night to end.

~

Pops was just walking out to the pool area with a tray of pastries as Will, shirtless and looking very much the worse for wear, stepped out onto the balcony outside his room and lit a cigarette. He squinted in the morning light, and walked back inside, reemerging moments later with Christie, who gave him a long kiss. Will took her hand and led her down the stairs.

By now, Pops had stopped at the top of the steps leading down to the pool from the yard.

"You know, it might be a little warm to be eating out here today," Karen said as she followed close behind her husband.

Pops didn't seem to know what to say. He wasn't sure how

his wife would react to their new guest.

Peri, who was following close behind her grandmother, swooped around her to grab a pastry from Pops' tray. "Score! I'm starving."

"Well," Pops continued. "I really think-"

Peri and Karen stopped short, for the first time seeing what Pops was seeing.

Will and Christie continued on around the pool, seemingly oblivious to their stares. Will kissed her again at the edge of the lawn.

"I'll call you later."

"Oh, that's okay," Christie said. "My boyfriend gets in tonight."

"Story of my life," Will replied without missing a beat.

Christie turned and headed toward the house as Will walked back to the group. He looked past Peri and his grandmother and noticed just the glimmer of a smile at the corner of Pops' mouth. Will reached for a pastry, took a bite, and arched his eyebrows at Peri before he started back up the stairs to his room.

Peri stayed planted in place for a moment, then hurried back to the house.

Jen flipped through a rack of clothing but wasn't seeing anything she wanted. Truth be told, her mind was only half-focused on looking at each item before she slid the hanger to the side and moved on. She was in a strange mood. She'd been short with James that morning, and had been slightly on edge since the moment she'd awoken. When Lucy and

Karen suggested a trip downtown to check out the boutiques, she'd hoped it might be a way to jolt her out of her mood, so she'd skipped her swim and joined them.

Now here they were, but it seemed her strange mood had tagged along with her. Her thoughts kept returning to one person-

"Do you think Will would like this?" Karen asked as she held up a blazer.

"I don't *know*," Lucy answered, in a way that suggested she *did* know, and the answer was *definitely NOT*.

"Well, I want to get everybody something. What about these two?" Karen continued as she presented a pair of coats – one white with clean edges, one black with roughly cut seams.

Lucy and Jen pointed to the dark one simultaneously. "That one," they said.

Karen tucked her chin against her neck and gave them both a look.

"Well. Okay then."

Jen exchanged glances with Lucy, then pirouetted to another rack of shirts as Karen walked over to her daughter and started speaking in a hushed voice.

One of the curious things about the family was that even when they whispered, no matter how improper the comments might be, they always did so at just such a volume that people could still hear exactly what they were saying. Jen couldn't help but wonder if this was intentional at times, but James had repeatedly assured her that it wasn't. Nevertheless, she could hear everything the two women were saying.

"Do you think everyone is having a good time?" Karen asked.

"I think so. There haven't been any major blowups yet."

"That's what I was thinking," Karen said. "The girls are the girls as usual, but Jen, Will, and James seem to be getting along."

Lucy's voice dropped still further. "Well, I don't know that they're getting along. They're just avoiding each other."

Jen walked back over, hoping to cut the discussion short. Lucy looked up suddenly, in a way that, assuming her voice had been hushed enough in the first place, would still have betrayed the fact that something sensitive was being discussed.

Karen pulled a belt down from the top of the nearest clothing rack and studied it up close. Her eyes sparkled with satisfaction. "Do you think this would be good for James?"

Lucy and Jen looked unsure.

Lucy brought a contemplative finger up to her chin as she debated her son's taste. "What's the price?" she asked.

Karen turned the buckle over so both of them could see.

Lucy raised her eyebrows, slightly stunned as the number registered. Then she and Jen answered in unison. "He'll love it."

"That's what I was thinking. I still need to find something to give your father at the big dinner next week."

"Do you have anything in mind?" Lucy asked.

"Nothing yet. I was hoping you could look with me."

"Yeah of course."

Karen turned to Jen, "We've been married for *decades,*

you'd think the pressure to find the perfect gift would ease up at some point, wouldn't you?"

Jen nodded her head, "It's understandable. It's a big anniversary."

—

Will had also taken the morning to wander around town. The market was open that day, which gave him an excuse to skip the family's trip to the beach and wander amongst the vendors instead. Smoke hung low under the canopies and pathways that crisscrossed the public square. The smells of smoked nuts, grilled meats, and warm pastries wafted past him, and his stomach groaned with hunger. He stopped at one of the stands to buy a ham and cheese baguette, and was just taking a bite when his mother, grandmother, and Jen appeared at the end of the aisle, each carrying a shopping bag.

He wasn't in the mood to deal with anybody at the moment, and ducked back, rotating his head and holding the sandwich up for cover. When he looked back, the three of them had continued on. He turned down an intersecting row, chomped into the baguette, and was just stepping out into the crowd of people when he nearly collided with Jen.

His mouth full of sandwich, he raised a tentative hand.

Jen laughed as he struggled to chew the mouthful of food.

"Hey," he managed finally. "How's it going?"

"It's going okay," she said with a smile. "You finding anything good down here, other than that sandwich?"

"Oh, yeah, yeah, couple nice things down this aisle." He motioned back along the way he had come. "Some stuff about halfway down the aisle that I think you might *really* like."

Will took a tentative step back.

"Like what?" Jen asked.

"Umm..." His mind had gone blank. He scratched the back of his neck awkwardly. "Spices?"

Jen laughed again. She had always liked Will best when he was knocked off balance.

"I'll check it out," she said.

An awkward silence set in, just a second or two, but long enough to catch them both off guard.

Jen raised her hand and attempted to say something relaxed before she headed on her way. "Well, I'll see you on the flip side!"

She turned on her heel and hurried down the aisle Will had just indicated.

I'll see you on the flip side?!

She smacked her forehead in embarrassment at her goofy exit-line.

Meanwhile, Will continued on through the market, crossing the street and heading down an alley of shops til he emerged by the port. All the while he shook his head as he mentally reviewed the play by play of what had just happened.

Jen stopped at one of the vendors' stands and looked at some satchels of herb de Provence. The stuff was everywhere, and clichéd and touristy as all hell, but just like always, she couldn't help but pick up a few more bags. Then she again heard two familiar voices and realized Karen and Lucy were once more behind her, looking at linen beach shirts.

"How do you think Jen and James are getting along?" Karen asked.

Jen ducked back behind a display.

"I honestly can't tell. I thought they were doing great when they first got here, but I haven't seen them together much the last couple of days."

"Well, your father and I could *hear them* the other night-"

There was a pause as Jen, and apparently Lucy, tried to figure out what she meant.

Jen felt her face flush as Lucy finally exclaimed, "Oh mother, please! I don't want to hear about that!"

"I'm just saying. It does seem like something is a little off now though, doesn't it?"

"Yeah," Lucy replied as the two of them moved on. "I've been thinking the same thing myself."

* * *

The girls and their husbands were spread out on the beach at Club 55, baking under the sun. The sky was clear. The water was calm. The crowd was gorgeous and *loaded*. In other words, it was a typical day. Peri and Tracie flipped through their weathered but little-read books, looking over the tops every five to ten seconds to see who was arriving on the motorized, inflatable skiff that brought the especially well-to-do customers from their yachts anchored offshore to the club boardwalk. It was coming up on lunchtime, and the boatloads of diners were coming in faster now.

Peri was holding a book with a sepia-toned cover of a brownstone. The title read:*"Two Nannies, Four Lovers."* Tracie meanwhile was reading a New York magazine with a picture of a rail thin woman holding a copy of the very same book, the headline trumpeted, 'Page Six's H. K. Griffin dishes on her fabulous bestseller.' Tracie looked over at Peri, who was watching the crowd coming and going from the dock, keeping her eyes peeled for celebrities.

"Anyone good today?" Tracie asked.

"No one big yet," Peri replied.

One of the inflatable speedboats roared away from the boardwalk, headed out to the waiting yachts, as another boat pulled in close to shore, spinning around in a tight circle as it moved in parallel to the weathered wooden walkway that sat about four feet above the waves. The captain steered the small boat closer to the metal staircase that extended from the dock down to the water, as an attendant on shore grabbed the boat and held it securely in place. The crowd of passengers – the majority of whom seemed to be slinky models and actresses of some variety – stepped off the boat and ascended the ladder, where they gathered in a circle, making sure everyone had made it off safely and all of their couture handbags and accoutrements were safely in hand. Then the entourage headed down the boardwalk toward shore. At the head of the group was a thirty-something guy dressed in linen pants, a pale blue shirt, and sunglasses. He was thin, slight of build, and not outwardly remarkable, but nevertheless, he seemed to be getting the lion's share of the women's attention.

Peri watched the entire scene carefully.

"Scratch that about 'no one big,' we just landed a whopper."

Tracie lowered her magazine. "Who's that?"

Peri, "You know that movie you saw last month?"

"Which one?"

"Any of them."

"What about it?"

"That guy produced it." Peri said.

Clayton dropped his copy of *Business Week* and looked up "Who are we talking about?" he asked.

"Jeff Pepper, "Peri replied as Clayton turned and watch the crowd walking toward the restaurant.

* * *

Will didn't even need sunglasses, he was already wearing a stylish, perfectly comfortable, entirely overpriced pair of designer limited editions, yet here he was, working his way through a spinner full of shades.

He let out a sigh.

He was feeling aimless. Maybe a swim back at the house would do him some good. He turned around decisively, ready to head back to the house, but instead, he ran right into Jen again, who was just coming around the corner.

"Oh," Will said dumbly. "Hey."

"Hey." Jen replied as she looked down at her hands.

Yet another awkward silence hung in the air.

"This is ridiculous," Will said. "Do you feel like getting a cup of coffee or something?

"Yeah, That might be good."

They found their way to a street café and sat at a table in a corner, away from the sidewalk and the din of the crowd. Will looked down at his espresso as he spoke.

"So, first of all, I apologize for the argument the other night."

"It was just one of those things," Jen said.

"It came on pretty fast though."

"They always did, Will," Jen said. "But that's old news. Lets talk about *now*. I've been reading the articles about you and what's her name?"

"Oh Jesus, you too?"

"I'm sorry, should I not bring up anything that's going on in your life?"

"Of course you can," Will said as he took a sip of his drink and met her gaze. "It just seems as though that's all anyone wants to ask me about anymore."

"And what do you tell them?"

"I say we had fun together. I wish her the best in life. She'll always be a part of mine. And I'm happy for her."

Jen narrowed her eyes now, the skin beneath her lower lids crinkling in just that way he remembered.

"And what do you really think?" she asked with a grin.

"What do I really think? Well, I never tell people what I *really* think."

"Tell me."

Will paused and cleared his throat quietly. He leaned forward.

"All right. We were together as much as two people in our

fields can be. Once a month or so, our schedules intersected somewhere. We'd have dinner, head back to our hotel room-" ...he leaned his head from side to side and arched his eyebrows ... "-then ten minutes later we'd both be on the phone to our managers. When we finally had a real vacation, just the two of us, we spent two weeks together and realized we couldn't stand each other."

"And why was that?" Jen asked without missing a beat.

Will pulled out his pack of cigarettes and put one in his mouth. Jen reached across the table and took one for herself.

"Why do people ever split up?" he asked. "Things change. I mean, why did it end with you and me?

"Didn't we just go over that the other night?"

"I know, I know. I just wanted to play music with my buddies, and you thought that was going nowhere."

Jen shook her head, bemused. "Well, I mean really, who knew Will Baker from back home would end up becoming... *Will Baker?*"

"You did. Once."

"Yeah," Jen admitted. "I guess I did. What happened?"

Will shrugged and cracked a smile to lighten the mood. "You've gotta admit, it's pretty cool the way things worked out," he said as he lit his cigarette and handed Jen his lighter.

Jen lit her smoke as Will took a long drag. He studied her for a moment, and exhaled a cloud of smoke.

"I've been meaning to ask you," he said. You're an editor at that magazine that's all about a 'balanced lifestyle' and whatnot. What's the deal with the smoking? They let you get away with that?"

"That's kind of the joke," Jen replied as she lowered her cigarette. "Everyone there is so worried about what goes into their food and their cosmetics and clothing, but they all smoke to stay thin."

"They *all* do?"

"Pretty much. James hates it." She paused, then continued, "Maybe that's why I still do it."

Will raised his eyebrows. "Okay, now see, that's a strange comment. Would you mind telling me what that means exactly?"

"Not particularly."

"I just gave you an honest answer to *your* question."

"Okay, okay," Jen said as she motioned to his clothes. "While you're being so honest, tell me this. Why do you wear so much black?"

"Easy. Because it goes with everything and it hides the places where I spill my drinks..." Will nodded his head emphatically. "Now it's your turn."

"What's the question?"

"How are things with you and James?"

"None of your business."

"None of my business?" he said. "My brother and my ex-girlfriend and it's none of my business."

Jen paused to take a sip of her drink. The cigarette remained clasped at a sharp angle between her fingers, leaving a wispy trail of smoke behind as she returned the coffee cup to its saucer.

"We're okay."

"Okay..." he dragged the word out. "Okay, like everything

is just fantastic, or okay, like, it's a marriage arranged by the state?"

"It's not a *marriage*," she snapped. "Look... I'm sort of uncomfortable talking to you about it."

Will seemed to ignore the comment.

"How did you guys get together anyway?"

"We bumped into each other at a party my publisher was throwing to celebrate the opening of The Gates in Central Park."

"Wow, very *nice*. Very *New York*. And he approached you?"

"Yes he did."

"And what was his pickup line?"

"He said, 'Didn't you used to date my brother?'"

Will slapped his hand on the table. "I knew it! He's never played one of my albums, but he uses me as his in."

"That didn't matter though. I recognized him before he said anything. I spotted him as I was coming in."

Will studied her rather closely. "But you didn't say anything? You waited for him to come up to you?"

"I could see in his eyes he'd be coming over sooner or later."

"And then what, you guys went for a drink?"

Jen was growing increasingly uncomfortable. She bit her thumb nail as she looked down at the table. "Yeah, we went for a drink, then he walked me home. The next morning we went down to the park and walked through the Gates like everyone else in the city."

Will considered pointing out the fact that she was skimming over a little period of time there. Avoiding a few key details, like whether or not James had come back to pick her up the next day, or if he had never left. It seemed the facts were there, unspoken, and in the end, he knew the ultimate outcome. But still, in those words, in the unstated facts, he had to admit that he felt a tinge of jealousy.

"You know, I was probably there then. I went to the park the next day too. The night before, I was at a party at 79th and Fifth."

"We were right across from you," Jen replied

"So then, you guys have been together like, a year and half? Have you moved in together?"

Her body language was growing rigid.

"We're talking about it."

Finally, he let out an exasperated question, "What's he *like?!*"

The intensity caught her off guard. "What do you mean?"

"I mean, what's he *like?* I barely know the guy anymore. I mean, is he a dork? Is he a slob? Does he drink too much? What music does he listen to?"

"He's fine. He drinks his share. I don't know that he's a dork. He works on Wall Street, I mean, the greed sort of cancels out the dorkiness after a certain point."

"What's he like to be with?"

She took a breath, glanced up at Will, then looked away a degree or two as she answered. "He's... clean. He's neat and methodical."

Even Will seemed surprised by the comment. "Wow, sounds charming. So, you're obviously head over heels in love with him then."

"I don't know what to say. It feels like I'm on the spot." Her eyebrows pinched together. "He's good. We're content. It's a relationship, what can I tell you? We spend most of our time together, you kinda lose perspective after a while. The other person's just, there, and you have a hard time picturing things without them."

Will tried to leave well enough alone, but he couldn't resist the chance to pivot to the past.

"You and I lived together. You seemed to have a pretty easy time picturing things without me."

"Will, you're talking about ten years ago-"

"Nine," he countered.

She turned back to him. Locking him in her gaze. "Look. I hate to tell you this, but it's a lot different than back then. We were kids."

The tone was changing fast. *Real fast.* Like Jen had just pointed out, 'it always did.' But Will couldn't help himself, even as he saw her eyebrows lowering, and noticed James walking down the street behind her – headed in their direction – he knew he was gonna end up pushing his luck. He always did.

"Well," Will said with a little smirk. "We weren't exactly kids. Remember how we used to-"

Jen's eyes started to open wide in a look of horrified, almost angry disbelief. She was just about to say something when James set his hand on her shoulder and she jumped.

"Hey you two."

She turned around in surprise. "Hey!"

The word came out just a hair too loud.

James leaned in and gave her a kiss on the cheek. "Hey, babe," he said calmly, before turning in Will's direction and giving him the most subtle, but seemingly all-knowing expression Will could ever recall receiving. "Will. How's it going? You two catching up?"

"Yeah, a little," Will said as he pushed the table's third chair toward James with his foot. "Have a seat."

James sat down and looked from Jen to Will and back to Jen.

"Have you guys kept in touch at all?" he asked.

Jen's voice sounded just a bit defensive as she said, "No."

An awkward pause hung in the air between the three of them until James lightly bobbed his head at Will with a smirk.

"Will, you still living at that house in Portland?"

"Yeah, when I'm off, that's what I've been calling home."

Will watched his brother, who nodded his head yet again, but was seemingly holding his tongue, waiting for Will to elaborate.

"I was trying the place in the city for a while, but after a few days it gets me antsy."

"Oh," James said. "You got a place in New York?"

"Do you think of any other place as 'the city?'" Will asked, an unfortunate tone hanging off the end of the sentence.

James either missed it, or ignored it.

"It's always a good investment," James said.

"That's what they tell me. So, what have you been doing down here in town?"

"Oh, Nekos was taking me around to some of the galleries,

showing me which artists were worth the money and which ones weren't."

Will slugged back the last of his espresso and stood up.

"Really? I was just thinking of going there before I bumped into Jen. Maybe we could all go down together."

James locked eyes with Jen, who was clearly uncomfortable with the idea.

"Yeah," James said. "Why not?"

~

Ten minutes later, the three of them were standing in a gallery down near the harbor. The midday sun was reflecting in off the water, baking the room in warm air within the shop's front windows. Jen walked across the room, her arms pretzeled over her chest, eyes cast down at her feet. The situation was making her uneasy, the unspoken tension between the two brothers set her on edge.

Even as kids, when she and Will had been dating throughout high school, and James was just the older brother who occasionally came home for college breaks to spend the majority of his time sitting on the couch watching MTV, she knew the two brothers had never really gotten along. They were siblings with a substantial age difference between them, in a single parent household. In that kind of situation, people grew up just a little faster, and the differences in their temperaments bubbled to the surface at a much earlier age.

She'd always had this image of James as being kind of a bore. Too interested in what other people thought of him, and almost afraid to set out on his own and be his own man.

He was the kind of guy who could never wear a funny hat, or do the funky chicken, for fear of drawing the attention of *anyone* in the room. You might say Will was the exact opposite, which is why, years and years later, it caught her by surprise when she suddenly found herself not just interested, but *attracted* to this guy she'd assigned to the back shadows of her awareness.

For the record, he was still too shy, still much too aware of what others deemed *cool,* but James Baker had really come into his own over the decade since she'd seen him last. Unfortunately, over the last year, as he'd really started racking up success on The Street, some of his worst tendencies had started working their way to the top, and with them had come a new level of trepidation on Jen's part. If she was being totally honest with herself, there *were* times that she found herself wishing for something more. In her relationship, and in her life.

Now here they stood – the three of them – in a warmly lit, richly decorated gallery. The musician and the businessman, with Jen between them. Studying artwork and inadvertently debating its value and why. And in her gut, even then, she knew which of them stood closest to her heart.

James was poised dead center before a tall black painting with a dripping red face that streamed down its center. Will stood off to the side, holding his sunglasses in one hand, a dubious expression tucked beneath his eyebrows.

"This is the painting Nekos was showing me this morning," James said. "He's got a ton of this guy's stuff."

"Who is he?" Will asked.

"How should I know?" James asked. "Some model probably."

"The *painter,*" Will replied as the most subtle of smirks passed over his face.

James seemed to miss the humor

"This one I believe is-" James studied a pamphlet in his hands. "Francois Paradis?"

"Ahhh..." Will nodded his head emphatically. "Francois...."

James looked over. "You know him?"

"No. I don't." Will opened his mouth to speak, hesitated, then stabbed his finger in the direction of the painting. "Do you actually like this?!" he asked.

"Yeah, I think it's amazing."

Will's eyes narrowed. He was dubious. "What about it appeals to you?"

"The guy is just amazing. He's really a master."

"Hmm..."

Jen, who had been pacing behind them nervously, decided this was the right time to walk over to where they were standing.

"What do you think of this one?" James asked her eagerly.

"It's all right."

"I'd like to buy it for you," James said.

"Oh no, I'm not sure its really my thing!"

"But it's an investment."

"James, please," Jen said. "I don't really want it."

"Really, you don't like it?" His shoulders dropped.

Jen stood frozen, then shook her head. "I'm sorry, it's just not for me."

James studied her for a moment, then reached for his wallet and headed for the front counter.

"Well, then I'm gonna get it for myself. I can't let a chance like this slip by."

Jen watched him go, then glanced in Will's direction, ready for him to give her a little look, or a curious shoulder shrug. Instead she spun to see him looking at a painting in the opposite corner of the gallery. He walked toward it slowly, like a crocodile sneaking up on a little red bird. He was giving her a break. She looked at the painting in front of Will. She liked that one much better.

~

After James had purchased the painting and finished making arrangements for its delivery to New York, the three of them walked down to the harbor, wandering past the yachts and the artists with paintings set up on easels for display.

Will pointed to one of the paintings as they passed. "Now, why didn't you look at one of these guys?" he asked.

"Who are they?"

"Who knows? Every artist starts out as somebody, or really, a nobody."

James curled his lip, clearly less than thrilled at the idea of paying for an unknown commodity.

Jen wandered over to another artist's display and started flipping through the laminated prints of his work. James walked up behind her, turning to look at one of the larger originals leaning next to the artist.

"How much is this one?" James asked.

The artist, an older man, looked up from under the brim of his large straw hat. "300 euro."

James raised his eyebrows as he lifted his Blackberry, checked the artist's name on the canvas, and started to type it into his browser.

Meanwhile, Will was standing at another booth, looking at an unusual painting of the harbor, one in which the buildings and people seemed to be melting and running into the water around the ships. He looked to the artist, a middle-aged woman reading an Agatha Christie novel. The book looked to be in English, so he hoped his halting speech would be understood.

"Bonjour. Uh, could you tell me when this was painted?"

The woman looked at the painting. "This one? Three years ago this August."

"Was that the summer you had the heat wave? When all those people died in Paris."

"Yes it was," she replied. "People died everywhere. Here we had heat and fires."

Will looked back at the painting. "Was everyone you know all right?"

"Everyone I know?" She nodded. "Most of them. The people I know were very lucky. There was one man, but he was very old."

Will studied the painting for a few minutes longer. "I'd like to buy this one," he said finally.

"Don't you want to know how much?" she asked

Will wobbled his head. He didn't give a shit about the

price.

"I'd like to have it either way," he said.

The woman seemed slightly thrown by this, but quietly took the painting down from the easel and began to wrap it up.

"It's nice to have someone ask about the work," she said finally. "Most people just want to know the price."

Will handed her his credit card and she took the information down on a charge sheet.

"Would you like me to have this shipped somewhere for you?"

"That would be great," he replied as he handed her a business card with an address.

Jen walked over to Will as he was signing a slip for the paintings, She arched her eyebrows and rolled her eyes in James' direction. He was on the phone, no doubt talking to Nekos about the painting. Will started to say something, but was caught off guard by a beautiful blonde-haired woman who walked past.

"Hey, Will," the blond said coyly.

"How ya doin'?" Will replied.

When he looked back at Jen, she was giving him a very odd look, one that he ignored as best he could as he headed back over to where James was talking on the phone.

* * *

The family had returned home for the evening, and the conversation revolved around the big sighting at Club 55 that day. Peri, Tracie, and Maureen were holding court at the kitchen table, alternately sipping glasses of rosé and filing their nails, while Arthur and Clayton leaned against the kitchen counter, checking their Blackberries and grazing on cheese and crackers.

"Listen to me," Peri said. "This guy's boat was *huge*. Bigger than anything we've seen so far. Clay, how much did you figure it was?"

"Few million, easy."

Will walked in from the patio. He took a bottle of Hoegaarden from the fridge and popped the top.

"And he came into shore with this entourage of like bodyguards and swimsuit models."

"Who are we talking about?" Will asked

Maureen looked up, feigning indifference. "Jeff Pepper. He's a movie guy."

"Oh yeah, I know Jeff. He directed one of our first videos."

Arthur's head shot up. "You serious, man?"

"I heard the guys a total asshole," Tracie interjected.

Will took a drink of beer from the bottle. "Where did you hear that? He's great."

The room grew quiet.

"Isn't he always directing and producing movies that bomb?" Maureen asked finally.

Clayton turned to her. "Hardly. I think he's had one *mild* disappointment since he started fifteen years ago."

Maureen rolled her eyes at that. "I heard his last one stank."

"His last project was '*Crackerjack*,' it's the number two highest grossing film of all time," Clayton countered.

Peri put her hand on her hip. "Well, then what's number one?" She asked.

"The *first* movie he produced," Will countered, as he took another sip of his beer and wandered out onto the back patio.

Jen was sitting by the doorway, having a smoke. Will felt around in his pockets for a pack of cigarettes, but came up empty.

"Can I bum one of those off you?" he asked.

"'Course you can. They're yours."

Will narrowed his eyes as he took the pack from her and shook one out. "How'd you get these off me?"

"I may be out of practice, but I still have the skills."

He considered taking that comment and running with it, but thought better of it. He needed as many people in his camp as he could find on this trip.

"Did you hear them in there?" he asked as he motioned towards the kitchen.

Jen nodded.

"Like I didn't say a word, right?"

"Oh, they heard you." She exhaled and studied the cigarette's filter. "Either Tracie or Maureen is always the first to speak when they want to marginalize what someone else just said."

"*Marginalize.* That's a little odd for a family, right?"

"In other families, yes. In yours it's the standard m.o."

Will leaned against the wall and looked out over the backyard. The light was going down on another day. The pink evening sky was reflected in the pool.

"Tell me how to deal with these people."

"Booze and women, Will. Booze and women."

"I've been trying that," Will said. "It doesn't seem to be working. Maybe I just haven't found the right-"

Arthur stepped through the doorway behind them. "Did Jeff Pepper really work on one of your videos?"

Will glanced at Jen and turned around slowly.

"Oh, yeah," Will replied. "He did a few of ours actually."

"I'm impressed, man."

Then Tracie's voice called out from inside.

"Who's making dinner tonight?"

Jen stood quickly. "Shit, I think I'm on duty."

She ducked inside a moment before Maureen came marching out.

"Will, have you cooked yet?" Maureen inquired.

"No I haven't."

"Well come on, we're all-"

Before she could continue, Will swept past her and headed into the kitchen.

Jen was already washing her hands under the faucet.

The kitchen began filling up with family members, as the color in the sky no doubt reminded them of the bottles of rosé chilling in the refrigerator, waiting to be uncorked. The volume of conversation grew as glasses were passed around, wine was poured, and the family filtered out onto the back patio.

While the crowd of family members was at its peek, Will slipped past Nekos and stood beside Jen at the sink. She was drying her hands as he reached in front of her to turn on the water and inadvertently brushed against her. When he'd finished washing his hands, he turned off the water and squeezed around behind her once more as he grabbed a washcloth. Just then, Nekos uncorked a fresh bottle of wine with a flourish, taking a big step backwards as he held the cork aloft in a sweeping arc. Will stepped forward to avoid colliding with his uncle, and wound up pressing his hands against Jen's back; they slid down to her hips instinctively, then dropped away, all but instantly. It was over and done with in a flash, but the moment lingered.

"Excuse me," Will said quickly.

Jen closed and opened her eyes once as Will dried his hands at her side, then they set to work preparing the meal.

"OK," Will said. "So what are we making?"

"I was thinking of a bow tie pasta with artichoke hearts and some grilled vegetables."

"That sounds... vaguely familiar," he replied with a smile.

It had been one of their staples during the time they'd lived together.

Jen nodded. "Old standby."

From *when* was something neither of them felt like pointing out.

"We used to be able to make that with our eyes closed," Will said.

He stepped to the left and pulled a pan down from the wall, then leaned back to the sink, filling it with water as he simultaneously threw in a dash of salt and headed for the stove. Meanwhile, Jen started rinsing vegetables and spreading them out on the countertop.

James walked inside, stopping in the main hallway. He

could hear the sounds of cooking and peered around the corner. The bulk of the crowd wasn't in the kitchen. He turned to the back patio and saw Maureen flipping through a magazine, a glass of rosé at her side. She set the magazine down, lifted her wineglass, then stopped to say something to someone out of sight. Then he heard another person's voice. The majority of the group was outside having drinks. It was Jen's turn to make dinner, so this might be the perfect time. He slipped his hand into his pocket, felt for the ring case, then headed around the corner and into the kitchen, where he stopped short at the sight of Will smashing a clove of garlic with the broad side of a knife. Jen was standing at the counter cutting up artichoke hearts.

James dropped the case back in his pocket and strolled into the kitchen, nodding at Will, who turned and scraped the smashed garlic into a cast iron frying pan.

James stepped behind Jen and set his hands down on her shoulders. She turned with a start.

"Hi," he said.

"Hi there," Jen answered, trying to seem relaxed.

"Sorry I keep startling you," James said. He looked over the cut up vegetables on the cutting board. "Looking pretty good in here."

Jen leaned closer. "I hope it is. Are you hungry?"

"Starved," he replied as he went in for a kiss. He pulled his head back and looked at her. "Have you been smoking again?"

"Yeah."

James paused as if unsure what to say next. From the

corner of his eye, he saw Will reach for something. The sound of sizzling olive oil soon followed. His brother had no doubt turned up the heat and splashed oil in the pan to blot out the roar of the awkward silence. James was caught by surprise at how greatly he appreciated the gesture. He looked at Jen, suddenly thrown off his game. He brushed his hands down the front of his pants. Felt his fingers again bump over the edges of the ring box.

Then, mercifully, Pops walked in.

"Smelling good, guys! Smelling good!" He looked at James, over to Will and Jen, then nodded and grabbed a bottle of wine as he headed for the door. "You kids seem to make a pretty good team."

James watched his grandfather leave and looked at Jen with a funny half smile on his lips.

She met his gaze.

James walked across the room without another word, took a glass of rosé from the table, and headed out to join the rest of the family.

Will toyed with the garlic as it browned in the simmering olive oil. If ever there was a time to leave well enough alone, this was it. At the moment, the merest joke or an impish smile would undoubtedly have sent Jen over the edge.

~

The dinner plates had been picked clean, even the ones his cousins had been eating from. Will noted that particular detail with more than a bit of satisfaction. It had no doubt killed them to so openly indulge in this particular meal so freely, but how could they not? It was a hell of a good dinner. Who could blame them for letting their bellies do the talking in this instance?

As the meal wound down, and after a particularly vocal recap of Long Island country club gossip had fully run its course, the conversation slipped into a momentary lull; even the cousins appeared to be at a loss for words.

Nekos reached for a freshly opened bottle of rosé, poured himself a glass, and made an announcement.

"James got himself a couple of tremendous pieces today. They should really make a nice cornerstone for his collection."

Lucy chimed in. "I was looking at the pics. They're beautiful."

"Very expensive pieces," Karen added with a nod as she glanced at her daughter and Jen. Lucy gave her a look, but made no further comment. Jen seemed uncomfortable.

Will on the other hand, perhaps feeling his oats from the success of the meal, had been a bit loose with his wine consumption. Looser than he normally allowed himself to get around family. His teeth were tingling ever so slightly. Never a good sign for things to come.

"All that hard work pays off I guess, eh James?" Will said

"Yeah, for some people it does," his brother answered. "Other folks just seem to get lucky."

Will flinched at this apparent dig, but he kept quiet at first. There was a good chance he'd started this one. Then, before he even realized he was going to say *anything*, he was speaking. And what's more, the tone of what he was saying was not good. Not good at all.

"What do you mean by that, James?"

"Forget it, bro."

Bro?

The only times he could recall James ever calling him *bro* had immediately preceded one of their more memorable fights.

"Bro?" Will asked.

"Boys," their mother cut in. "Let's not do this tonight."

"It's okay, Mom," Will said. He locked eyes with James now. "What did you mean by that comment?"

"Nothing," James answered. "Forget it, all right. I was just talking about how things work out for some people."

"You think I haven't work hard?"

Now Pops could see where this was going and cut in a little louder, *"Boys, please."*

James flexed his jaw, his cheeks rippling gently. "Let me put it this way," he said. "You never made higher than a B your entire academic career."

"Bullshit, James. I aced every art class the high school offered."

"Yeah, art," James said with a laugh. "Art doesn't matter."

"Mattered to me." Will took a sip of wine and reached for the bottle to refill his glass. "And it must matter to someone you're trying to impress, or you wouldn't have shelled out all that cash for those paintings today."

Pops stood and walked away from the table, disgusted.

The cousins seemed entranced by the conversation.

"I think you're missing the point," James said.

"I don't think so. I see exactly where you're going with this."

"And where is that, Will?"

A fork clinked against porcelain as Lucy pushed her plate away.

Will stopped himself. "Nah, forget it."

"You think I'm jealous of you?" James mocked. "Jealous of the rock star?"

"I think you resent me a little, yeah"

"What's there to resent?" James asked.

Lucy and Karen started clearing dishes from the table.

"It doesn't bother you at all how things have worked out for me?"

James locked eyes with Will. "No."

Arthur and Clayton headed for the pool with their Blackberries.

"Well that's good then. That's great."

"Honestly," James huffed. "I pity you."

"You *pity* me?"

"Look at you. Yeah, you've got money. You're famous-"

Jen stood up quickly, her chair screeching on the patio floor as she stormed away.

"But who cares?" James continued. "Who gives a shit when you're just a drunk, with no family, no girlfriend, no one who gives two shits about you."

"No one who cares?" Will almost laughed. "What the hell are you talking about? I've got *plenty* of people who care." He glanced around the table then, quickly realizing that only Tracie, Peri, and Maureen were remaining. That struck him as quite funny. "Okay, yeah," he said with a sort of veiled smile. "Maybe I'll give you that one for the moment." He exhaled a soft laugh. "I don't even know why we're having this argument."

"I don't know why either."

James seemed to be relaxing a little now.

Unfortunately, Will just couldn't leave it alone.

"Really," Will continued. "Isn't life too short for this sort of childishness? Just do me a favor, will ya? Just settle down for a second, take a deep breath… and go fuck yourself."

James was blindsided, his mouth hanging open for a moment, then he jumped to his feet as the words sank in.

"Fuck you too, Will! Fuck you too."

James walked away, leaving Will sitting with his cousins. He looked around at the bunch of them.

"Yep, I'm the asshole. I know. I'm the asshole."

He stood, grabbed the remainder of the wine, and walked away.

~

Jen was at the sink washing her face when James walked into the room. He walked across to the armoire, pulled the ring case from his pocket, and shoved it into a duffel bag in the upper cabinet. Jen turned off the water, dried her face with a towel, and climbed into bed as James watched her. She flipped off the lights and lay on her side with her back turned to him.

James sighed. "Why are you pissed at *me?*"

Jen said nothing.

"What did I *do?*" he asked.

"Don't be a jerk."

"So you're mad at me. Great, are you mad at Will too?"

"I'm *annoyed* at Will, but I'm not here with Will. I'm here with you, so yeah, I'm mad at you. Will was being just as big a jerk as you, but you're the one who started the whole thing."

James sat crouched on the floor.

That wasn't entirely true.

"It's not that big a deal," he said.

"Why? Because he's your brother and you've always argued like this?"

"Yeah, actually. And besides, I don't know how this is any of your concern anyway."

Jen sat up and faced him. Her face and form glowed milky white in the light shining in through the windows.

"It's my business when I see you acting like a jerk. You're jealous of him. Anyone can see that. You're jealous of his money. You're jealous of his homes. You're jealous of the women he's been with-"

James cut her off, "That's ridiculous."

"Is it? Then why are you with *me,* James?"

He inhaled slowly. Trying to calm himself. "Don't even go there."

"You just had to take a cheap shot at him tonight. This isn't Wall Street, James. This is your family. You don't take a cheap shot at family to get them down to your level."

"I can't help it if he starts asking for it."

"Oh give me a break. That's the sort of thing your cousins would say."

Jen turned and dropped her head to the pillow.

Her mind was racing, her pulse quickened.

She stared at the shadows on the wall and listened to the sounds of guitar music strumming from the pool house across the yard.

* * *

Jen was lying on a towel in the sun. The family, minus the cousins and Will, was scattered around the shadow of Karen and Pops' beach shelter. It was another gorgeous morning at Club 55, before the crowds of notables and the unknown power players would start roaring into shore from their yachts in the harbor. The beach was still cool, slightly damp with the residue of late night condensation. Jen squeezed the sand in her fists, enjoying the sensation as it clumped together in the contours of her hand, then slowly dried and crumbled around her fingers.

She looked around the group. James was checking emails on his Blackberry. The two of them hadn't exchanged more than a few words since they'd gotten up that morning.

Nekos was thumbing through his latest paperback thriller. Jen lowered her head to check out the title: *Billionaires, Bullets, Exploding Monkeys.*

She shook her head.

Ridiculous pulp garbage, as usual.

Arthur and Clayton were sitting side by side, reading the papers out of London.

Their phones rang simultaneously, and like actors in a Tweedle Dee and Tweedle Dum skit, they reached for them at the same time.

Jen looked toward the water as she heard their voices droning in the background.

"What?" they mumbled together.

"Wait, *what?*" Clayton said on his own, just a tad louder.

James' chair creaked as he turned to see what was happening.

"What is it?" James asked.

Then *his* phone rang.

Now the family was starting to look around. Jen and Lucy crossed gazes. Lucy raised her arms to ask what was happening. Jen shrugged her shoulders.

"You're kidding me," James said into his phone.

"Holy shit!" Arthur shouted.

"WHAT?!!" James bellowed into his own handset.

Then a moment later he and Clayton were yelling together, *"Holy shit!"*

James was struggling to his feet now, his free hand compulsively drawing up to his head, scratching at his hairline. "OK. OK. Let me think. I'm gonna be on the next flight out of Nice. I'll call you from the car."

Arthur and Clayton were on their feet now too, scrambling to gather their towels and shoes and newspapers. Sand was flying everywhere.

Nekos had dropped his paperback. "What in the hell is going on?" he asked.

"The market's tumbling," James said. "We have to get back to New York."

"You're kidding me," Nekos exclaimed as he started to

stand.

"Nekos!" Anne said as she reached out a hand and grabbed her husband's forearm.

"How bad is it?" Nekos asked.

Clayton had his hand over his cell phone's mouthpiece. *"Bad,"* he muttered.

"What flight out should we take back?" Nekos asked.

"Nekos, you're not taking any flight," Anne said. "You're retired."

Nekos narrowed his eyes, looking from the guys to Anne and back to the guys.

"Either way, we have to get back there," Arthur said.

"We'll drive you," Anne said as she got up from her chair.

⸺

The ride back to the house went quickly. Jen looked at James, gauging how he was doing. They still hadn't said much, but jumping into action together during a semi-crisis seemed to have pushed them past any awkwardness.

When they got back to the house, James ran upstairs to get his things together. Jen had been tempted to go with him and head back to the city at the same time. It somehow seemed funny to be hanging around with his family in France if he wasn't going to be there for a few days. There was a good chance he might not even be able to return to Saint Tropez before the trip was finished.

Karen, no doubt reading Jen's mind, stopped her in the hallway as she was starting up the stairs.

"Jen, listen to me, there's no reason for you to cut your trip short just because James has to go. We want you to stay here."

"I feel like I should be with him-" Jen said.

"For what purpose?" Karen interrupted. "Take it from one who has been there, you'll just sit there, listening to him on the phone, wishing you were still here. Let the boys go back and do their thing, we'll stay here and enjoy ourselves."

Jen stood in the kitchen, listening to the sounds of people packing in other parts of the house. It took a few moments before she realized she wasn't actually alone in the room. She jumped with a start when she looked over and saw Sara, looking a bit the worse for wear, slumped at the table, snoring softly.

Pops walked past the doorway and looked in at her, wordlessly giving her the thumbs up as he headed for the stairs, where James was coming down with his bags. He was talking into his cell, but covered the mouthpiece as he looked up.

"They convinced your girl to stay," Pops told his grandson.

"Oh yeah?" James replied. 'That's great." Then he picked the call up right where he'd left off. "Yeah, we should be in the air in two hours. We'll get in this evening."

James, still on the phone, walked out of view as Arthur and Clayton rushed into the front foyer with their own luggage in tow. They had no sooner tossed their bags on the floor, than Peri, Maureen, and Tracie walked through the front door, shopping bags in tow, looking around in confusion.

"What's going on?" Tracie asked.

Nekos walked around the corner, car keys in hand. "The

boys are leaving. We gotta deal with the market."

Anne called in from the kitchen. "Your Uncle isn't going anywhere, but the rest of the boys have to go back for business."

Nekos, still determined to take part in the action, chimed in, "I'm driving them to the airport now."

"If all goes well, Clayton said, "We'll be back in a week."

"Well, have a good trip I guess," Peri muttered as she wandered away from her sisters and their husbands.

Clayton leaned over and gave Maureen a kiss, "We'll be back before you know it."

Jen and James stood together on the patio outside the kitchen. She gave him a hug.

"I'll see you in a week," he reassured her.

"Have a safe flight."

He looked her in the eyes. "Are you still mad at me?"

Jen gave him a sheepish smile. "We're fine."

Lucy walked outside carrying a small paper bag. She studied her son and his girlfriend, apparently deemed things 'OK,' and piped in. "I made you a steak sandwich for the plane. Take it. You'll thank me. Trust me."

"Thanks, Mom."

A car horn blared from the front yard. Jen drew back, visibly tensing at the sound.

James picked up his bags and hurried for the door. In the commotion, no one noticed his Blackberry, which slipped from his shirt pocket as he bent to lift his luggage. The car horn started honking again and he ran for the door.

"Have a safe flight. We'll see you soon," Lucy called after them.

Jen stood on the patio, watching James as he ran out to the van. Nekos waved from the driver's side window.

Jen crossed her arms and watched as the car pulled away from the house, leaving her behind, along with the way things were.

~

Morning came too soon, as always.

The early light hit Will's face as he descended the stairs and crossed the lawn toward the main house. He held his hand up over his eyes to shield them from the glare, and dropped it to his side the moment he passed into the shade of the trees that ran on either side of the yard.

He walked into the kitchen and saw Sara slumped at the kitchen table. He'd been up much too late, and had drunk far too much. If her past exploits were any indication, she'd been off doing the same thing.

His stomach was pinched in hunger. He reached for a croissant, took a bite, then slumped his shoulders and dropped it back on the pastry tray. In the balancing act between nausea and hunger, the hangover was winning out.

"I can't eat," he grunted, half to himself and half to Sara.

His cousin looked at him with a deathly slack-jawed expression, and said nothing.

"You hung over too?" he asked.

Sara let out a gurgling moan that he took to mean 'yes.'

His stomach was apparently unprepared for solid foods, but his head needed something. Coffee for sure. Maybe a little orange juice, depending on the degree of pulp. He trudged over to the coffee maker and poured himself a mug.

"I met this hot French guy at the club last night," Sara said weakly.

Will took a sip of his coffee and turned to listen, but that was apparently all she had to say.

"Where is everybody?" he asked after a few moments.

"You missed the excitement."

Sara again sat in silence. Will looked at her expectantly.

"Look, Sara, French guy is self-explanatory,' Will said. "'Missing the excitement' is something else. Are you gonna tell me what happened?"

Sara shook her head gingerly. "I thought I just did. I'm sorry, my internal and external monologues just aren't computing today. The guys all flew back to the city this morning."

"The city?"

"The market took a nosedive and they freaked."

"Really? So, who are we talking about? Arthur, Clayton, and James?"

"Yeah. My dad wanted to go too, but Mom said 'No.'"

Will took another sip of his coffee, trying to modulate the interest in his voice.

"Did anybody else go with them?" he asked.

"You mean, did Jen leave too?"

Will narrowed his eyes.

Sara met him squint for squint.

After a moment she let him off the hook. "Jen's still here."

Will said nothing, just reached for a croissant. He took a feeble bite, dropped it back on the tray, and leaned against the kitchen counter.

"She's with your Mom at the beach in case you were wondering," Sara continued by way of explanation.

Will glanced toward the doorway as Pops walked by, carrying someone's Blackberry. One of the guys had no doubt left it behind in the rush to get to the airport. Will watched his grandfather as he headed up the stairs.

It must have been James'.

He turned back to Sara, who was staring at him again, a sickly smirk spreading across her face.

"Save it," Will said. "Don't look at me. Where is everybody else?

"Some are at the beach, some are downtown," his cousin replied. "Like I said, *Jen* is at the beach."

* * *

Another night, another meal. The dinners piled atop one another until each blended into the last, and you couldn't recall if that *delicious* pigeon (yes, *pigeon*) had been served at the vineyard from the night before, or three meals prior, or if that mouthwatering fish had set off fireworks with the rosé at Bar Sube, or with the chardonnay in that bistro atop the cliff outside town.

Tonight they were in Ramatuelle, a village set atop a steep hill at the end of a long, winding roadside thirty minutes outside Saint Tropez. According to the chatter in the kids car on the way over, the family had been to this particular village for one or two dinners before Will's arrival, but this was the first time they'd been able to snag a reservation at this particular restaurant, which all of the girls had heard nothing but raves about. They'd made sure to request a particular table that looked out to the water in the distance, and their success in obtaining a reservation for their party had put the cousins in a surprisingly chipper mood.

Will sat in the van, surrounded, yet alone; Sara had taken the opportunity to nab James' vacant seat in the grown up car. When they finally stopped in the lower parking lot, without the adult van anywhere in site, Will climbed out the side door and waited for the cousins to lead them to supper.

It turned out the lot was actually quite a ways below the final destination. The group, with Will taking up the rear, trudged up the hill and around several side streets, before they came to the restaurant. Once they had arrived, Will noted the location of the adult van with a half smile; the rest of the family had found a parking space less than 20 feet from the main entrance. Were he not standing there, the three cousins would no doubt have taken that opportunity to fight amongst themselves in assessing who was to blame for the sore feet they'd just developed in the course of their trek up from the car. Instead, they stood in simmering silence.

Will held the door for the group, then he followed them in, where they found the rest of the family looking around the building's unusual interior. Save for a couple of tables that sat along the balcony at the far end of the building, it seemed the entryway led almost directly into the kitchen. Preparation tables were lined up against one another, running the length of the room. Ovens and gas stove tops were set into the wall to the right, with a half dozen kitchen workers stirring pots, lifting lids, and sliding dishes into the heat. To the left sat what looked to be two wood-fueled stone ovens, with dutch ovens set among the coals and hung from cast iron hooks that hovered over the flames.

Will glanced at Nekos, who shot him a half smile and arched his eyebrows, as if to say, *'We're in for some surprises!'*

Will shrugged in what he hoped would come across as an easy going 'What can ya do?' gesture.

When a waiter walked over and started leading the rest of the group toward the *oven,* Nekos again turned to his nephew, this time shooting him a surprisingly alarmed look of apprehension.

"Follow me, and please, mind your footing on the stairs," the waiter said in a thick French accent as he pointed to an amazingly narrow set of stone steps that hugged the side of one of the ovens before plunging down and around the oven's chimney and base, descending into the dimly lit floor below.

Will watched Jen approach the stairs first, she looked back at his grandparents, clearly concerned that one of them might lose their footing on the steps behind her. Then the cousins, Anne, and Nekos followed behind.

"Does this make anyone else think of Hansel and Gretel?" Lucy asked.

Will took to the stairs, feeling the soles of his shoes slipping on the well-worn steps. A fall on these things would be treacherous. He spread his fingers wide and pressed them against the walls on either side. As he approached the bottom, the light on the stone took on a soft pink glow. Then he rounded the corner and found himself in a covered dining area, filled with scattered tables that led out to an open patio. The view beyond the rail was *spectacular!* The sun was just starting to set on the horizon, casting the view of the landscape in picture-perfect Provence light.

The crowd murmured. The climb up the hill, then back down the stairs had been more than worth it.

"This is *gorgeous*," Karen said.

"Fabulous," Anne added.

"Goddammit!" Nekos shouted.

Anne spun in her husband's direction, a flabbergasted look flashing across her face. "Nekos!"

"Look over there," Nekos whispered as he nodded in the direction of a table in the far corner.

Anne followed his gaze until she saw what had set her husband off. There in the corner -- she with a butter knife in one hand and a half-buttered roll in the other – he with a soup spoon clenched between his teeth, hands clasped on either side of his head -- sat that same angry German couple they had been encountering at just about every meal.

"Everyone, just ignore them," Anne said. "Don't pay them any attention."

"Unbelievable," Pops whispered under his breath.

The rest of the group tittered amongst themselves as they pointed out the nefarious couple. They all took their seats as Will walked over and sat between his mother and Pops. He watched Jen circle the table, carefully selecting her own seat. He had briefly contemplated sitting down beside her, but considering the present company, decided it was better to play it safe, lest the more chatty members of their party take it upon themselves to point out awkward moments and inconvenient proximities. A busboy came over and began filling their water glasses as the waiter handed out menus. Will studied the selections as he cast occasional sidelong glances in Jen's direction. She seemed to be studying her own menu closely, so he focused his determination on *not* looking her way for as long as possible... Until he did, only to find that she was looking him straight in the eyes. Time hiccuped. The motions around them slowed, sounds slipped into the distance, his family's voices fell away, and it was just *them*. In the cone of swirling motion around them, Jen and Will locked eyes, and smiled. Then time picked up where it had left off, and the crowd around them began chatting and laughing again. Jen looked away, and Will followed suit.

~

The flow of the conversation moved differently at the evening's meal, largely because the cousins had free rein over much of the available airtime now that their husbands and James had headed home. Will spoke with Sara a bit across the table, and glanced in Jen's direction now and again, but there was never a comfortable moment for them to switch places or strike up a conversation.

A dozen bottles of wine and a few hours later, dinner was done, and the crowd rose from the table and headed up the narrow stone staircase to the upper level. Will stopped at the foot of the stairs and turned to Peri.

"I'm just gonna run into the bathroom real quick," he said. "I'll meet you guys out there."

She gave him a wordless look and continued upstairs.

Will ducked towards the waiter station in the back of the room, and one of the servers waved him to the restrooms in the back of the dining area.

Jen was in the middle of the group as they reached the upper hallway. She noticed a series of photographs hanging in the lobby and walked over to check them out as a few of the family members headed up the street to get the car. The rest walked out to the front sidewalk.

Jen studied a few of the photographs, looking at each for a moment, then moving on to the next. Her eyes were drawn to an image at the end of the line, a view of what looked to be this same restaurant when it had apparently been a private residence. It must have been taken decades earlier. She moved in closer, examining the shot of the fitted stone interior carefully. Then she noticed the expression of a little boy in the lower left hand corner, and leaned down to examine his face. It seemed familiar somehow. When she turned away and looked back in the direction of the kitchen, she realized why. A heavyset chef with short black hair tucked under a white fabric cap stood at the edge of the counter. His manner, the quality in his eyes, and the way he bit at his lower lip, were all the same as the young boy in the photo. She assumed he must be the owner.

Something about a family member living and working in the same location, the same *building,* all these decades later, struck an unfamiliar nerve with her. She couldn't imagine it. Her own life had been filled with so many continually changing settings and players that the idea of lifelong continuity left her with an almost jealous ache.

Jen opened and closed her eyes slowly.

She blinked and looked around.

The lobby was suddenly empty.

She hurried over, pushed the heavy wooden door open, and walked out on the stone pathway leading to the old brick street.

There was no one there.

She glanced up the street, in the direction of the adult car she'd arrived in, but the van was gone.

She jogged halfway up the street and looked around.

No one.

They couldn't have left her. Could they?

She stood in the middle of the street, listening for the sounds of the car. Surely they were circling back to pick her up. She had no idea where she was, or how to get back from here.

All she could hear was the rustle of a gentle breeze, and a dog barking in the distance.

She headed back down the street to the restaurant, stopping in surprise as Will walked out of the restaurant's front door. He was looking around in much the same way she had just done. Bewilderment hung heavy on his face.

"Where is everybody?" he asked.

"They're not inside?" She was still hoping for a misunderstanding, but preemptively anticipating his response.

Will shook his head as his mouth fell open slightly.

"You've gotta be kidding me," he said. "I told Peri I was running to the men's room and would be right out."

"You don't think they forgot us?"

"They must be going to get the other car before they come back for us," Will said.

Jen shook her head. "No sign of them yet."

She stepped back and stood next to him, waiting.

Another minute passed. Nothing.

"You rode with the girls, right?" Jen asked. "Where did they park?"

"In a lot down the hill a little ways," Will said.

"Maybe they're waiting there?"

"We can try," he said with a shrug.

They stepped off the curb and headed down the street. Neither of them spoke, as if they were afraid to break the silence and scare off their potential ride home. When they got to the bottom of the hill, where Will and his cousins had gotten out a few hours earlier, the lot was empty. Save for the flickering glow of a buzzing, bare bulb that hung from a powerline overhead, the area was pitch black.

They exchanged looks.

"Think they might be headed back to the restaurant?"

Jen narrowed her eyes and threw her arms out to her sides. "Probably not, but what have we got to lose, right?"

They headed back up the street.

Again, there was no one in sight. The lights in the restaurant were now out, and the doors and shutters had been pulled shut.

"Maybe they have a phone we can use," Will said hopefully.

As if on cue, the roar of a car engine rumbled up from behind the building. The noise grew louder and louder, then a bright yellow Ferrari came tearing out of a back alley. Jen looked in the driver's seat and recognized the now grown boy from the photo – the owner of the restaurant was behind the wheel, burning rubber outta there. A waitress was sitting in the passenger seat. The driver gunned the engine as the waitress screamed in delight. Then the car tore out of the alleyway, fishtailed on the stone roadway, and disappeared into the night, tires squealing in the distance.

Jen and Will watched in silence.

"Guess he had something else cooking," Jen observed.

Their shoes made a muted scratching sound as they padded over to a stonewall that ran alongside the walkway in front of the restaurant.

"I guess we just have to wait for someone to realize we're missing and come back for us," she said.

"You really think that's gonna happen?" He didn't see that as a possibility.

"I have no idea," Jen admitted.

Will sighed and sat down beside her as they waited in the warm night air. Off in the distance, the sounds of music played softly in the summer night.

~

When the owls started hooting and the wind picked up, they agreed that help would definitely *not* be on the way.

"Let's find a phone," Jen grumbled as Will followed behind her. Their footsteps echoed on the cobblestone streets, but Jen's agitated clip set her a few paces ahead of him.

Will knew the sound of that stride.

She was pissed.

They continued on in silence for several blocks.

"Where do you think we'll find a phone?" she asked finally.

"Not a clue. Do they even have payphones anymore?"

Will watched Jen out of the corner of his eye. He'd seen her angry many times over the years, and it was never pretty. The passage of time had not dulled the more pointed memories of Jen's most enraged moments, instances that usually developed as a result of something *he* had done wrong. Even now, knowing for a fact that he was in the clear, he couldn't entirely shake the impulse to hunch his shoulders and wait for her to let him have it. He looked around uneasily, studying the darkened windows along each side of the street.

"Seems like everyone has gone to sleep," he observed.

Jen walked on, not uttering a sound.

"Are you pissed at *me* for something?" Will called after her.

"Of course not," she called over her shoulder.

Wait a minute, *was* she pissed at him? He knew that tone all too well.

"You know, this isn't my fault."

"No, it's not," she said. "But it would sure be easier if you carried a cell phone."

"Wait. *What?* Why don't *you* have a phone?"

"Because I'm wearing a dress. You've got on cargos."

Will looked down at his well-pocketed pants. The truth was he never carried a phone with him if he could avoid it. Even if he did travel with one, he always inadvertently left them behind somewhere, abandoned on a shelf or table when something or some*one* stole his attention away. There was a drawer at his house in Portland where the cleaning ladies had thrown all of his deactivated and returned handsets over the years. Instead of a junk drawer full of rubber bands and take out sporks, he had a drawer full of phones.

"This is ridiculous," he said. "You can't honestly be trying to pin the blame on me. I'm not even gonna get into that-"

"Fine," she said, cutting him off.

"Good."

A cat rushed past the two of them in the darkness. Will watched it pass, it's white fur briefly blooming under the glow of a streetlight.

"I knew I shouldn't have stayed here," Jen said.

"Now, what does that have to do with any of this?"

"I just should have known this kind of thing would happen."

"That's ridiculous."

"Thanks!" Jen shot back testily.

In years gone by, that might have shut him up, but Will plowed ahead.

"You know what I mean. You've just gotta try to forget about...*them* and enjoy the rest of the trip... and the rest of the walk." That brought a slight laugh. "I have a feeling we're not gonna be finding any payphones on the way back."

~

The air was warm and surprisingly humid. Jen hadn't noticed this before tonight. Maybe it was the company, or the situation, but the atmosphere seemed to grow thicker as they walked down the road, alongside the innumerable vineyards. They were just coming to a bend in the road, passing under a canopy of trees that dropped lazily overhead in the darkness, when a breeze blew through and whispered over her skin. The chill of the air felt good as it swept away some of the tension and left them in its wake. Her skin tingled with goose bumps.

As they came around the corner, the road split off in two directions. Neither option looked at all familiar to her.

"You think town is that way?"

"That seems right. I guess." Will said.

He had been silent for much of the walk.

Jen peered through the rows of grapevines that stretched out into the distance, where they seemed to intersect with a road on the horizon. She followed the path of a lone pair of headlights as they wound around and disappeared into the night.

"Think that's the same road over there?"

"I have no idea." Will followed her gaze. "It seems like it might be."

"Think it's worth cutting through here somewhere?" she asked.

"I don't know if that's such a good idea." Will said.

"It might save us time. This road curves around so much, I bet we could knock off at least an hour."

Will still seemed uncertain. His eyebrows were pulling together and up in the middle, the way they did when he was anxious about something. In years gone by, that was when Jen had always decided for the both of them.

She stepped off the road and headed for the rows of vines.

"Executive decision," she explained. "You can follow me if you like."

Will lifted his arms in resignation. "Well, that doesn't leave me much choice, does it?"

He rushed to catch up to her as she walked on, looking up at the night sky, where the moon was glowing through a formation of billowing clouds.

"It's amazing out tonight," she said.

"Looks like Halloween to me," Will said as he looked up at the sky. "Does Saint Tropez have serial killers?"

"Every place has serial killers."

"Terrific."

They walked a ways further, until they came out in an open pathway between the rows.

Will stopped and tried to get his bearings. He pointed into the distance. "I think town is that way," he said.

"How do you know?"

"I can just feel it."

"You feel it..."

She'd been led astray one too many times by Will's gut instincts.

"I might have told you this before," Will explained, "but guys have an innate sense of direction. Scientists have put male and female mice in a maze and-"

"Oh God! The mouse story. I remember. I remember. *Please* don't tell me the mouse story again."

Will looked at Jen, his face almost in silhouette, two white eyes blinking back at her.

"It's true-" he protested.

She pivoted on one leg. "OK, so we've got to head that way then."

She started on ahead, again leaving Will to hustle and catch up with her. He looked around uncertainly as the sounds around them grew more pronounced the farther they moved from the road. Then they were in the middle of the vineyard. The moon shone down through the fast-moving clouds overhead. Something rustled off to the side and disappeared among the vines.

Shit.

He had never liked walking anywhere in the dark. His imagination got the better of him. He feared things, like killers, and animals, and that spectral sea captain he'd read about in a book of New England ghost stories.

At least Jen was here.

An owl hooted in the distance and Will's steps staggered in response. His heels shuffled in the gravelly soil, causing Jen to look back over her shoulder at him.

"You're not getting scared are you?" she asked.

He didn't respond, just kept on walking.

She glanced back at him again and smiled.

She knew he was nervous.

Dammit.

They continued on for a ways as the wind picked up and the clouds raced over them faster and faster. The air was getting cooler now as it blew past. Then, as they reached the end of another row, a house appeared in the distance. Jen caught her breath softly. The two of them walked on in silence, afraid to get their hopes up. When they reached the edge of the fenced property, they found that all of the windows, even those around the side of the building, were pitch black. Will walked closer, resting his hand on the wooden crossbeams that ran along the length of the fenced yard. Every ten feet or so, the wood rails came to rest on a stone pillar, before continuing on for another ten feet.

He looked at Jen, "Think anyone's home?"

"Looks pretty dark to me."

Will motioned toward the fence.

"What are you gonna do, break in?" she asked.

"'Course not. It's just a long way around this yard. I thought we could save some footwork if we cut through. Remember *Holiday Inn?* It's a shortcut to the shortcut."

"Don't they end up in a lake?"

"That's...true," Will conceded.

Jen looked at the house, then up and down the length of the fence. "I think it should be okay," she said finally.

"Great. I'll help you up first."

She rolled her eyes. "Fine."

Will walked behind her and wrapped his arms around Jen's waist to lift her. He started to hoist her up, his stomach pressing against her back as he did so, but she squirmed away, turning and pushing her hands against his chest.

"Yeah. That's okay buddy. I can do it myself."

Will feigned innocence. "I'm just trying to help."

Jen put her hands on the top rail of the fence, then leapt up and over it in a single, smooth movement. She touched down on the other side, turned and waited for him.

Will hesitated, then reached to the top and started to pull himself up. He grunted loudly and slid back to where he'd just been.

"Shit," he muttered. "I shouldn't have had that last glass of wine."

"You mean bottle?"

He gave her a look. "Thanks."

He gave it another go, letting out a long, slow groan as he reached the tipping point and slowly rolled over the top. He landed on the other side, hard.

"Jesus, Will," Jen said as she helped him up. "You might try shelling out for a trainer.

"Again, thanks," he said as he dusted himself off. "You're doing wonders for my self-esteem."

They started across the yard. Looking from side to side as they got their bearings. A dog barked in the distance, followed by another of those disconcerting rustling sounds.

Will froze. "What the hell was that?"

"I don't know," Jen replied as she looked over her shoulder.

Suddenly, a torrent of barking enveloped them as they turned to see three Dobermans tearing across the yard toward them at full clip.

"Oh shit!" Will shouted as he and Jen took off running.

The dogs were close on their heals, their fangs glinting out from the darkness as moonlight hit their saliva-slathered incisors.

They made a beeline for the opposite fence as the dogs

quickly gained ground. Jen reached the crossbeams first, set her hands on the railing, and sprung over the top. Will followed close behind, and had just started to follow suit, when he was abruptly pulled back to the ground as one of the dogs bit down on his pant leg and pulled him backwards. Will fell to the dirt, where he kicked the dog away, and scrambled back to his feet.

His momentum stolen, now he'd never get over the fence before the dogs were on him.

He made a 90-degree left turn and started running along the fence line as the other two dogs continued the chase. He hit the far corner and threw up his arms, running and jumping at the perpendicular section of fence, his hands grabbing the rail top as his feet kicked and scraped beneath him for traction. Finally, he pulled himself up and over, only to find himself tumbling head over heels down a steep hillside on the other side! He yelped in surprise, his arms and legs flailing uncontrollably as he tumbled down the stony hill. Finally, he landed in a ravine at the bottom, where he lay face up, staring at the clouds overhead as they drifted away, once more revealing the full moon.

Will lay on the ground, catatonic. His face scratched and bloody. His ears ringing.

The clouds rolled overhead, and his eyes opened and closed slowly. One moment the sky above was clear, the next it was covered with clouds that pulsated under the moonlight. He drifted in and out of consciousness, unsure how much time was passing. Then he heard footsteps moving toward him, and looked up to see Jen's face leaning down in front of the moon.

"Are you okay?" her voice echoed.

He tilted his head gingerly to look at her. Tried to speak, felt his lips moving, but heard no sound.

"Will!" Jen yelled.

She brushed dirt and pebbles from his forehead, and the haze slowly lifted.

He blinked and raised his head.

Still he moved his lips, but again, nothing seemed to be coming out. It took a few more attempts for him to actually form words again, then the sounds around him – the night breeze, the owls, the barking dogs atop the hill, and frogs croaking in a nearby brook – all of it rushed in on him, along with the weary, confused sounds of his own voice.

"What the hell happened?"

He sat up and looked around.

"You just took a huge fall," Jen said as she reached out a hand to keep him from sitting up too quickly.

Will rubbed the back of his neck as he looked up the side of the steep hillside.

"Well," he said woozily. "I didn't see *that* coming."

He climbed uneasily to his feet and stretched his back as Jen watched him.

"You think you should be moving?" she asked.

He groaned and ran his hands over his arms and legs.

"Nothing seems broken. I think I can make it."

She looked unconvinced. "I can't believe you're all right."

He glanced at the hill again, then dusted himself off for the second time that night.

"Neither can I actually."

Getting their bearings was going to be a little tougher now. They were at the bottom of a steep ravine. Though the moon was full, and only occasionally obscured by a few clouds that continued to race overhead, there was no other source of light in the vicinity, and the steep sides of the lowland setting compressed the available moonbeams to a dim blue sliver.

"Well, so much for shortcuts," He muttered. "Where in the hell do you suppose we are now?"

"Just like before, I have absolutely no idea. It took me forever just to find a way down here to get to you."

Will made circular motions with his pointer finger as he studied the fence at the top of the hill and tried to calculate how it related to the dog-eluding path he'd followed along the fence line above just a short time earlier.

"If I jumped over that wall, and we ran to the fence from across the way, I assume we can just follow the ravine this way, and see where it comes out."

"Ohh-kay," Jen answered. Clearly at a loss for an alternative navigational take on things.

They started walking, but Jen still kept a close eye on his tentative gate. Will had to be hurting after that tumble. She would never tell him as much, but she was impressed he'd taken such a brutal fall with such élan.

"You're *sure* you're okay?" she checked one last time.

"Oh yeah," he answered, almost immediately tripping over his own feet and staggering to stay upright. Jen reached out and grabbed his arm.

"I'm fine. I'm fine," Will assured her again as they headed

into the shadows of the ravine.

—

It was impossible to gauge the time out here, but hours must have passed as they trudged along, slowly making their way up to higher ground and continuing on through more vineyards. Will was still limping, which made the going a little more difficult. Jen could hear him taking short quick breaths whenever he took an unexpectedly deep step or tripped over something underfoot. Finally, he broke the silence with a question.

"So, what about you?"

"What about me?" Jen said.

"We've talked about my love life this week. What about yours?"

"Mine..." she trailed off.

"I've heard the whole New York story about you guys meeting, and it was special and touching and all that, but, what about the nitty gritty. What is it that keeps you two together?"

"Nothing 'keeps us together,'" she said defensively. "We have our own lives, but we just... fit I guess."

Will arched an eyebrow.

"Okay then," she said, turning the tables. What kept you with what's her name?"

"Her body among other things."

Jen's lip curled. *"Honestly?"*

"We're not talking about me here."

"What keeps any couple together? It's just a good

arrangement."

"Arrangement. So you're like, living in a Merchant Ivory movie then?

"We've got chemistry. Don't sell it short."

Will laughed. "Yeah, I can see it now, wild sex every Tuesday night between repeats of the Gilmore Girls and One Tree Hill."

She scowled. "As a matter of fact we-," she stopped short. "Do you *watch* those shows?"

"No," Will snapped.

Jen eyed him until he shrugged.

"Even a rock star can't go out *every* night."

They walked in silence for a distance before he spoke again.

"Tell me this then, how is this a more adult relationship than what you and I had?"

"Well for starters, we act like grown ups."

Will made a slide whistle sounds. "Oh really? In what way?" he asked suggestively.

"We take responsibility. We have respect for each other."

"Personally, I like being *dis*respected, if you know what I mean."

Jen sighed. "You really don't change, do you?"

"Not if I can help it." He paused, then continued. "So you stick with it when things get difficult-"

"Fuck you, you know I do."

"Ooh, okay."

"Don't even try to go there again."

"I'm sorry," he replied quickly. "I was just messing around."

They walked on again in silence.

Will arched his eyebrow at her again.

"Hey, Jen. Do you remember when we used to-"

She was still mad, but smiled a little in spite of herself. "I remember. I think you wrote a song about that, didn't you?"

"A bunch of my songs are about that- and you."

"Including one really mean one."

"Which one, *Mischief Night?*"

"Yeah, I think that's the one. I really wish you'd stop playing that."

"Are you kidding me? They'd riot if I stopped playing that song. It's one of our biggest hits."

"But it's so... angry."

"Half our fans are angry. Angry, bitter, jilted lovers. Or at least they think they are."

"But it makes me look terrible," Jen said. "Like I'm this heartless woman, or was..."

"What can I say? It was honest."

She didn't respond.

"Does it really bother you?" he asked.

"Lets just say that if I'm in a bar and that song comes on the jukebox, it gets very uncomfortable if anybody there knows who I am."

"Well I'm sorry-" he started, but Jen cut him off-

"It's like a full frontal assault on me. That's like your only song with insane swearing in it."

"Yeah. I guess it probably is.

"And you wonder if that bothers me?"

"Look, I don't think either one of us wants to get into that stuff again. I think you've said yourself a couple of times that

it was nine years ago."

Jen looked down at the ground and started to walk faster.

Will hurried to catch up. The lights from downtown were beginning to inch over the edge of the hillside ahead of them.

"I'm sorry that a song I wrote when I was 21 is popular and still gets played, but I can't apologize for writing it. That's something that happened to me, and I think because its real, it strikes a cord with people. I wrote plenty of other songs about you too."

"When did you stop?"

"Stop?"

"Writing songs about me."

"Who says I did?" Will asked.

"What are you telling me, that you didn't write any songs about what's her name, or any of those other girls you've dated?"

"I may have, but you know, people choose their audience, and they write and perform to that person. I wrote *Mischief Night* cause I wanted to get back at you. But I wrote tons of songs when I wanted to get in your pants, or win you back."

"Do you really think of me when you write that stuff?" she asked.

"Sure I do."

She stopped and looked at him. "I'm not sure how I feel about that."

He shrugged. "Not much I can do about that."

"Which songs?"

"I'm not gonna tell you that. It could be about a woman, or about a boat. Words can get switched around, but the emotions are still tucked away underneath."

"So wait, I'm a *boat*?"

He tilted his head at her. *"Please."*

She started walking again. "Let me ask you something. Have you been avoiding your family because I'm with James now?"

"Of course not," Will sighed. "You've seen my cousins. *They're* the reason I avoid family gatherings."

"You say that, but I don't know that I believe it. I've seen you with your grandparents, and I know you're close with your mother. Actually, you're close with *everyone* except the cousins. I have a hard time believing you'd let them keep you away from the people you care about."

He was quiet for a moment. "I don't think it's worth talking about."

"See, you prove my point." She said. "So what is it that you're avoiding? It's me, isn't it."

Will hesitated.

"No."

"Is it James?"

"James and I were never close."

"Never?" she asked.

"Well, maybe after Dad died. But that was a different situation."

Jen watched him closely.

"Remember that summer I lived up at the college with you?"

"You're changing the subject?"

"Yeah," Will admitted. "I am."

He watched Jen to see if she'd play along. After a moment she turned her head to him expectantly, waiting to see where he was going with this.

"Remember that bar we used to go to on the weekends?"

"What about it?" she asked.

"I don't know. I just always think about that place when I think about us. Do you recall the band we used to go to see there?"

"You mean Richard Kimball and the Fugitives?"

"Yeah," Will laughed. "The lead singer looked exactly like Stephen King!"

Jen smiled down at her trudging feet. "They were pretty good."

"Sure better than half the sessions musicians we've auditioned over the years! What do you suppose ever happened to those guys? Think they're still playing?"

"I doubt it. They're probably all retired... or dead."

"Really? Those guys seemed to love to play though. I think about them a lot when I'm up on stage. The way the singer would just smirk to himself and stumble around a little, like he was just totally into the music."

"That's because the bar paid those guys with drinks."

"That was a great year. We went there every week I think. Then we'd walk that road back to the apartment, and I'd stop and lean you against a tree and-"

Jen's mouth drew tight. "That was a long time ago."

Will continued. "We'd lie out under the moon for a while, just making out, then we'd go back to the apartment. Remember?"

Jen stopped and looked at him, smiling ever so slightly. Her eyes sparkled in the moonlight.

"I remember."

"Remember how we used to-"

"Of course I do." She bit down on her lower lip. This was dangerous ground. "But I remember a lot of other stuff too. You know, I didn't just end things because I couldn't handle all the good times we were having. There was a lot of crap we had to deal with. We weren't always so happy."

"Are you happy now?" Will asked.

"Well," she paused the find the words. "I'm sure not sad."

"You don't seem happy to me."

"And neither do you," she shot back.

Jen turned in the direction of town. They had made it to the outskirts of the port. It must have been after midnight, yet people were still out and about, partying in the playground of the rich and famous. After their walk through the wilderness, and the accompanying memory trips back through time, it seemed dawn should be coming on fast and strong, but the wee nighttime hours were still at hand.

They started walking again.

"What do you suppose is missing?" Will said after a while.

"Nothing. No relationship is perfect, feelings dim a little, things don't fit together like they used to. Some relationships are more like yours and mine. And some are more grown up. Some have passion, some don't."

"Passion." Will said the word like a question.

"The thing about passion is that it fades. Passion isn't built to last."

"But it keeps life interesting. It cuts to the heart of things. To your feelings."

"It cuts to the heart," Jen agreed. "But a stake does that too."

Will opened his mouth to speak, a Van Helsing joke on the tip of his tongue, but he thought better of it.

The noises of the night rustled around them. Music was whispering to them through the alleys and side streets. He took a slight step forward, but stopped as Jen grew tense. He took a step back, and her eyes closed slowly.

"You wanna go into town for a drink?" he asked.

Her lips closed gently. She was either swallowing an imagined sip of wine, or taking a moment to regain her composure, Will wasn't sure which. Then she looked up at him, eyes wide, and sparkling in a way he remembered all too well.

"Yeah," Jen said. "I *would* like a drink."

* * *

The walk into town was just a bit longer than expected. On a number of occasions they had to cling to the old stone walls that ran alongside the twisting narrow roadways, for fear of being taken out by speeding cars as they slalomed down the hills toward the port.

As they approached downtown, the music and the crowds doubled with each block they walked, until they found their way to the outside of a particularly down and out looking bar. Without saying a word, they made a beeline for the entrance. The two of them had always shared a taste for the more slummy of local hangouts, and this one looked to be no different. As they mingled with the crowd en route to the bar, Will motioned to a free table in the corner and shouted over the noise.

"You still order the same thing?" he asked.

"Yeah!"

Will raised his arms and cut sideways through the crowd til he sidled up to the bar and caught the bartender's attention.

"Gin martini. And I'll have a bourbon. Best you've got."

The bartender nodded and set to work making the drinks.

Jen looked up a few moments later to see Will making his way to the table.

"What's that?" she asked as she nodded at his drink.

He held it under her nose as she took a whiff. Her face puckered.

"Bourbon?"

"Purely medicinal. It warms my vocal chords."

"Uh huh, and you're planning some performances while you're here?"

"No, but trust me, it brings benefits over time."

"Well aren't you mister health conscious," she said with a smile.

Jen took a sip of her martini and surveyed the room. She turned back to see Will setting down his glass, now empty. He motioned to the bartender for another.

"Holy shit, Will. Drink a little?"

"Only way I get by."

She studied his expression to see if there was any truth to

his bard boiled banter.

"How much do you drink?"

"Much as it takes."

"Stop the Robert Mitchum routine, will ya? You ever drink on stage?

"Sometimes."

"You drink in the studio?"

"Always."

"Why?"

"I told you, it relaxes the vocal chords-"

"Yeah," Jen cut him off. "I don't buy that."

"Okay then, don't buy it."

"Ever get sick of it?" she asked.

"Sure, but that's what drinking's about, wearing yourself out so you can put up with things."

Jen leaned forward, resting her temple against the tip of her finger, with the other fingers curled up next to her cheak. "Ever tried recording an album sober?"

"I did the whole last album sober, everybody hated it."

With that, the bartender arrived and set a fresh, full glass before him. Will took a drink and leaned back in his seat. A moment later, the room came alive with murmurs. Jen and Will turned to see what was happening, only to observe a man in his 30s, accompanied by a bevy of gorgeous young women, making his way through the crowd. A group of muscular men, bodyguards no doubt, were walking the perimeter alongside them.

Jen recognized the first guy immediately, she couldn't recall his name at the moment, but it was sitting right on the edge of her tongue-

"*Jeff Pepper!*" Will exclaimed happily. "I *heard* you were in town."

So, Jen thought to herself. *This* is Jeff Pepper. He must have been right around Will's age. Maybe just a few years older. Either way, the dude was obviously very young to be oh so very rich.

"I was gonna say the same thing to you," Pepper replied as he stepped forward, shaking Will's hand as he set his other hand on his shoulder. "You still on tour?"

"Just finished actually."

Jeff studied Jen from the corner of his eye. " Just you and the lady on this trip."

Jen blushed.

"Oh no, we're not together," Will replied. " Not anymore anyway."

"Whoa," Jeff laughed. "Bad trip I guess."

"We dated a long time ago." Jen said quickly and perhaps a bit too loudly.

"Together again for one last week of passion then, huh? I've been there."

Will started to speak, but Jeff slapped him on the back.

"I'm just messing with you man. What are you drinking? Why don't you put a couple rounds on my tab and join us at our table?"

"You cool with that?" Will asked Jen.

"Of course."

They got up and started walking through the crowd. Just as they approached a table in the far corner of the room, a camera flash went off. Will was slower to respond to it, but Jeff spun reflexively as the light rippled through the room. He nodded his head in the direction of a young guy with a camera who was doing his best to slip back into the crowd. Two of the men from Jeff's entourage, along with two guys from the bar, stepped forward, put their hands firmly on the cameraman's shoulders, and led him out of the bar.

Jeff yelled into Will's ear, "They been sneaking in on you wherever you go?"

"It actually hasn't been too bad here," Will replied. "The only ones trying to manhandle me are the girls."

"And that's never a bad thing," Jeff laughed.

"I'm sure you've got your share of admirers, what with the money from that whole attack shark laser-tag movie."

Now Jeff was laughing. "That was pretty dope, right?"

Will just smirked.

Jeff's voice rose in alarm. *You didn't like it?!*

Will was able to dodge the question as one of Jeff's guys walked over, gave his boss a nod, and directed them to a deep booth in the far corner, where the group proceeded to settle in.

Jen noted the way the girls in Jeff's group seemed to shuffle and position themselves in an effort to sit next to him. If Jeff noticed any of this behind the scenes jockeying, he did a good job of outwardly ignoring it.

"Hey!" Jeff exclaimed as he sat down. " We're having a little shindig on the boat tomorrow afternoon. You guys should come."

Jen nodded her head, her enthusiasm catching even her by

surprise. "That would be great."

"Nothing big really, just a gathering of friends. Little hedonism. But just a bit."

The word hedonism must have tickled the fancy of the girl sitting closest to him, as she started whispering in his ear and tugging on the collar of his shirt, leading Jeff out of the booth toward the dance floor. He put up a mock struggle, then reached out his hands to another of the women and motioned for her to join them.

"You two care to join?" Jeff asked.

Will looked at Jen and shook his head no. She just gave him a fun little smile.

"I think I'll sit this one out," Will said.

But Jeff wasn't even listening. Before they knew it, the music had picked up, the lights in the room had started spinning, and everything around them seemed to get swept up in a wave of pumping music and pulsating lights.

~

Though it felt like just a moment had passed, several hours later, Jen looked across the table and realized they were seated in a fairly quiet bar. She watched Jeff Pepper as he alternately nibbled on the necks of his two dancing companions. They were all clearly drunk now. In the dim of their corner booth, Jeff was methodically unbuttoning the first girl's top.

Will and Jen exchanged glances.

Time to go.

Will took the lead and stood up. "Jeff, we'll catch you tomorrow man."

Jeff looked up, seemingly startled to realize other people were still seated at the table with them. "You guys leaving?" he asked, as he pulled his hand from the girl's shirt and reached over to shake Jen's hand.

Will stepped in and intercepted, patting Jeff on the shoulder. "Catch ya later man!" he said jovially, though he was clearly exhausted.

"Tomorrow," Jeff replied. "We'll see you tomorrow."

"See you tomorrow," Jen said softly as they moved quickly for the exit.

* * *

Will and Jen were sitting in the kitchen the next morning, wide-awake with the awful and seemingly unavoidable morning angst that came after a night of drinking. Pops sat at the end of the table, reading the paper and drinking his coffee. Jen and Will flanked him on either side, staring down into the mugs of black liquid before them, and holding their heads in pain.

Lucy walked into the room and started drying the dishes and silverware. She tossed a handful of forks into the utensil drawer and slammed it shut hard.

Pops lowered his paper, looked in his daughter's direction, and turned to Will, who was recoiling at the deafening reverberations bouncing around in his tender head.

"Your mother's upset with your cousins for forgetting the two of you last night."

Will looked up, still holding his head. "Mom, its fine. We made it home okay. Still managed to have some fun."

"Too much fun," Jen gurgled into the crook of her elbow as her head slid down and collapsed atop her arm.

"That's not the point," Lucy replied. "It just says something."

Will laughed. " I think that's gone without saying for a very long time."

Lucy turned back to the sink and continued cleaning noisily. Her shoulder's tensed at the sound of the cousins' voices coming down the hallway. Peri was the first to pop her head around the corner.

"Hey guys, sorry about the misunderstanding last night."

Will couldn't help but crack a smile. "No problem," he said. "We bumped into some old friends downtown as we were heading back to the house."

"Oh yeah," Peri asked with forced indifference as she caressed a croissant on the pastry tray. "Anybody we'd know?"

Will recognized a certain tone in Jen's voice when she chimed in.

"Well, I didn't know him, personally, but I think you've heard about Jeff Pepper being in town."

Peri snatched up the croissant and shoved it in her mouth, chewing through pursed lips. "Oh yeah?" she said as a burst of damp crumbs popped from her mouth.

Pops, who had been reading his paper, lowered the pages and looked in their direction. "Jeff Pepper, the movie guy?" he asked.

Will nodded. "We're going to a get together on his boat this afternoon."

Peri turned and walked out of the room. Muttered exchanges could be heard in the outer hallway as she no doubt filled Tracie in on this latest irritating turn of events. The front door slammed. Then, nothing.

Lucy, Will, and Jen exchanged glances. Pops raised his newspaper and exhaled a long, deep sigh.

* * *

Will and Jen made their way through the crowds that mingled with the artists around the harbor. They stopped at the boarding ramp for a small yacht with the name "Apocalypse Sun" emblazoned across the back.

"This has *got* to be Jeff's," Will mused.

Jen's faced registered horror. "He *made* that movie?" she asked, disdain simmering on the tip of her tongue.

"Yep, and that movie made him."

They stepped up onto the ramp and made their way to the back of the yacht. A female crewmember greeted them at the top.

"Hi, we're here to see-" Will started.

"Welcome aboard, Mr. Baker," the woman interjected.

"Thank you."

He was accustomed to the inexplicable but understood phenomenon of perfect strangers recognizing him and addressing him by his last name, but he couldn't help but look in Jen's direction to see what her reaction would be. She seemed somewhat taken aback. That was refreshing to see.

"May I take your shoes?" the crewmember asked them.

"Certainly," Will replied.

"Oh sure," Jen said as she slipped off her shoes and gave Will a questioning look.

"They damage the wooden decks," he explained.

The crewmember led the two of them along a side platform and around the cabin to the front of the ship.

"We'll be heading out to the yacht in a few minutes," their guide said.

"This isn't the yacht?" Jen replied. The tone of her voice let Will know she was duly impressed.

"This is Mr. Pepper's ferry to and from the mainland," the crew woman answered.

Will made a very conscious effort *not* to look in Jen's direction at that comment.

A moment later a waitress emerged from a door that exited from the side of the cabin. She was carrying a silver tray with two shot glasses, two champagne flutes, and a bottle of Dom Perrignon. She stepped forward and held the tray before them.

"Compliments of Mr. Pepper," she said.

Jen smiled and motioned toward the green liquid in the two shot glasses.

"What is that?" she asked

"This is absinthe, madame."

"Absinthe?" Jen looked to Will. "Isn't that supposed to work like a corkscrew through your brain or something?"

"That was always one of the rumors, but I'm sure they ran this stuff through a coffee filter or something first."

Jen looked from the glasses, to the waitress, and back to the glasses.

"Thanks, but I think it's a little early for me."

The waitress raised the tray slightly.

"I'm afraid it's one of Mr. Pepper's requirements before we leave port. He likes to be sure people arrive to the party *ready* to party."

Will arched an eyebrow and reached for one of the glasses. He raised it before Jen's eyes. "Well, a man's gotta do what a man's gotta do."

Jen watched as he tilted the shot glass back and gulped the drink down in two swallows before whipping his head from side to side in an effort to shake away the aftertaste.

"Blech!" he belted out. Then he reached for one of the champagne flutes, which the waitress quickly filled up.

"Oh God," Jen gasped as she felt her stomach tensing at the thought of such an ill-matched combination of drinks.

"We'll be heading out shortly," the crewmember said as she filled the second champagne flute and handed it to Jen. "Have a great afternoon," she said as she walked away with the second, still full glass of absinthe.

"You okay?" Jen asked Will as they walked along the railing.

Will held him stomach in silent agony. A moment later, the ship sounded its horn and started pulling out of port. Jen stood at the rail, watching a crowd of children with ice cream cones, who waved to them from the dock. She waved back at them happily. As for the childrens' parents, they pretended not to notice the ship's departure.

Jen left Will leaning against the rail and headed toward the bow of the ship, where she looked down at the hull cutting through the water below. Once they hit the middle of the harbor, the ship began moving in a slow turn towards the open water, setting a direct course for a *massive* ship that was waiting out in the middle of the deep, azure water. They approached in a wide arc, coming in from the offshore side of the ship and gently pulling up to the stern, where members of the ship's crew, dressed in white pants and red shirts, were waiting for them. They quickly pulled the boats alongside one another to allow Jen and Will to disembark. As soon as they had stepped off, the smaller of the two boats began gently pulling away. One of the crewmembers led them along a walkway and over to a set of stairs, where he motioned for them to go on ahead.

The two of them climbed the stairs uncertainly. Jen could tell that even Will was slightly taken aback by the size of the yacht.

He looked over his shoulder at her and whispered, "I knew he was doing well, but this is *ridiculous.*"

They reached the top of the stairs, only to find Jeff Pepper waiting for them, another bottle of champagne and two more flutes held in his hands. Jen could see this was a losing battle.

"Welcome aboard! Welcome aboard!" Jeff said as he handed each of them a glass.

"Thank you for having us" Jen blurted out, then ducked to avoid getting hit by the cork as Jeff cracked opened the champagne and started filling their glasses.

When he'd finished pouring the drinks, Jeff pivoted in the direction of three beautiful young women who emerged by his side. One of them handed him yet another partially filled champagne flute, which he then proceeded to top off and tip back.

Jeff waved his hand in the direction of the closest girl, a thin brunette in a light summer dress. "Will, I'm sure you remember Becca from my Christmas party-"

Becca stepped forward, smiling as she gave Will a seductive kiss on the cheek.

"Hi, Will," she said softly.

Will nodded. "Hello."

"And these ladies are Skylar and Gem," Jeff added. "Girls, this is Will Baker and his friend Jen."

Jen looked slightly irritated as Skylar stepped forward and ran her hand down Will's chest.

"Nice to meet you," she said.

Gem smiled shyly and whispered, "Hi there."

Will caught Jen's gaze as she mouthed the name, *'Skylar??'*

Both girls kept their eyes on Will for a moment, then they shot a look at Jen, who raised a tentative hand. "Nice to meet you."

Jeff led them across the deck. "So, you'll probably recognize some people on board. If you need anything, just ask for it, or take it. The ship is all yours."

"Thanks again for having us," Jen said.

Will thanked Jeff and turned to the girls. "Maybe we'll see you ladies later."

"I'm sure you will, Will..." Becca said.

Jen crinkled her nose. Where did Jeff find these girls?

Like mythological sirens, the three women started running their fingers over Jeff's shoulders and arms as the four of them walked away. It was as if they were gently coaxing him across the deck. Supple, tanned Olympic curlers of seduction.

Left alone once again, Will and Jen walked out onto the massive deck. There was a pool in the center, and topless women were scattered everywhere, laughing and joking, or hanging over one handsome man or another, each of whom was either sharing a drink with them, or talking on a cell phone, oblivious to the female attention. Everyone was drinking. Loud music thumped in the background.

"I'm gonna need another drink," Jen said.

Will was already leading them to a bar alongside the pool.

"Me too," he answered. "I'm not sure I knew what we were in for here."

~

The afternoon slipped by quickly. Moving faster with each trip to the open bar. Soon the visible soundwaves of soft music and laughter were skittering through Jen's vision, tracer-style, as her head lolled from side to side drunkenly.

It was a curious sensation to exist in the middle of the crowd but, owing to her own inhibitions and personal boundaries, not to mentioned her concealed breasts, be rendered all but invisible in this sea of debauchery. Everywhere she looked she saw couples horsing around in the pool. Groups of people sneaking away to dark cabins. Or darkly tanned playboys lounging in the company of two, three, or four women, but never less than one.

Will had disappeared, leaving her feeling all the more awkward and vulnerable. He'd been swinging by to check on her fairly regularly, but seemed to have gone AWOL. Jen could only imagine what he was up to at the moment. She sat alone at a table, adjusting her outfit and trying to look casual as she struggled to determine how many of these little coconut cocktails she'd consumed in the last hour. By any estimation, it had been a lot, but she couldn't begin to guess her ratio per hour, as the face of her watch had long ago dissolved into a Dali painting.

Finally, she decided to get up and test her sea legs. No sooner had she taken a step, than she realized her ocean-going equilibrium, questionable as it had been at the start, had now been rendered non-existent. A waiter passed with a tray of tequila shots and Jen snatched one up without thinking.

Tequila!

That was just the ticket.

Little juice in the system to reset the ballast.

She didn't even know what she was thinking, but thoughts were burbling through her cortex nonetheless, and that made her laugh.

Jesus, was she ever drunk!

Jen giggled and held a hand to her brow, blocking out the sun as she looked across the deck and spotted Will and Jeff leaning against the railing, peering out over the water. She started to walk toward them, but a nearby chaise was suddenly calling to her. She dropped to her knees, crawled across the deck, and slowly but surely clawed her way on top, where she promptly fell asleep.

~

"I'm telling ya," Jeff said. "If these cousins of yours are so impossible, you should just borrow one of my motorbikes and tool around the shoreline on your own."

"You serious?" Will asked. "Cause I just might take you up on that."

"Do it! I'll send you home with one today."

"Yeah, Will," a voice whispered. "Do it."

Will turned to see Becca and Skylar standing behind him. He looked at Jeff, who cracked a broad smile as the girls stepped around Will from either side and started kissing him on each cheek. Then their siren hands were on him, drawing him toward the interior of the ship.

~

Jen blinked under the softening pink sky. She had no idea where in God's name she was now. She blinked again, and the pink cloud above her slowly shifted into focus. Sharp, painful focus. She sat up and nearly fell forward on her face. Her head moved with the agility of an unbalanced pile of rocks.

From the look of the light, it was late afternoon, and the party had entered its mellow period. The partiers on the deck had apparently shifted into make out mode.

There was no sign of Will.

Jen stumbled to her feet and began making her drunken way towards the ship's main cabin. She rounded the corner and found herself in a hallway, which led to a series of doorways. She took a left at the first of these doors and headed inside, only to stumble back out again as the sounds of shouting voices chased her away.

~

Will, Becca, and Skylar were stretched out on a bed in a dimly lit cabin. There was a pulsing red light, which reminded Will of the glow from the lava lamp Jen's freshman year roommate had kept running twenty-four hours a day in their dorm. That thought was still crossing his mind when Becca moved forward and kissed him on the mouth. Then Skylar kissed him on the neck, just behind his ear. Then Becca and Skylar kissed each other. Then Skylar leaned over and kissed Will on the lips as Becca unbuttoned his shirt. Will stared up at the ceiling, letting things coast, unsure what was happening or why. He heard the sound of a latch opening and closing, but it didn't entirely register in his mind.

By now the girls had moved further along. Skylar was doing something to his earlobe with her teeth. Becca lolled to the side and giggled as something caught her attention.

"I think your friend wants to join us," she whispered.

At first Will thought "friend" was a euphemism, then he looked toward the doorway and saw what she meant.

Jen was slumped against the door of the cabin her glazed eyes watching them.

"Jen," Will blurted out as he tried to spin his legs around and climb off the bed. Instead, his feet got tangled in his pants and he tumbled off the side and out onto the floor.

"Oh God," Jen muttered as Will struggled to his feet.

She turned and rushed out of the room.

Will looked at his companions, stammered to speak, then waved his arm in frustration and ran out of the cabin.

The girls watched the empty doorway for a beat, shrugged, and began making out.

Jen swerved back and forth across the deck, evading Will's attempts to stop her. Finally, she slammed into the deck railing, leaned her head out over the water, and threw up over the side.

"Are you okay?" Will asked.

She held he head in her hands, trying to pull herself together.

"I'm fine," she whispered. "I'm fine."

Will put his hand on her back.

"I'm so sorry," Jen said. "I had way too much to drink. I don't know what I was even doing back there."

"There's nothing to be sorry about-"

She groaned and heaved over the side again.

"Let's get you home," Will said.

"No, no. I'm fine. I'm fine."

"Jen, you're saying everything twice. You're not fine."

He rubbed his hand on her back, waiting to see if she'd get sick again. She was breathing quickly, trying to catch her breath as she wiped at her mouth on her shirtsleeve.

"I haven't been sick like this in years," Jen said.

"Too busy acting like a grownup I guess," Will said in a way he hoped would come across as lighthearted, but the words hung in the air. "I get sick like this at *least* once a week when we're on tour."

Jen didn't laugh, or say anything, she just let out a soft moan.

Will waited a bit longer to see if there would be any more

alcohol coming back up the hatch, but that seemed to be all of it. Jen straightened up slowly, and Will moved in and put her arm over his shoulder. They were just getting to the top of the stairs that led down to the lower deck, when Jeff came wandering out of one of the cabins. His shirt was unbuttoned, his hair noticeably disheveled. Jen leaned her face against Will's chest.

"Jeff, we've gotta head back to shore. Jen isn't feeling well."

"I'm sorry to hear that. Too much fun?" Jeff asked.

Jen sighed weakly and nodded her head.

"It looks that way," Will said.

"Well, take care of her. It was good seeing you guys." Jeff shook Will's hand, then added, "Hey! Make sure you get one of the bikes when you get to shore."

Will looked at him, cocking his head at an angle. "You're definitely sure about that?" he asked

"I *told* you it was okay man!"

"Thanks. We'll be seeing you again then."

"Course you will!" Jeff said as he headed back inside.

Will and Jen continued down the stairs and onto the smaller boat, which was waiting to take them to shore.

* * *

The ride back to the house wasn't easy, not with a drunken passenger clinging to Will's back and failing to compensate for any of the turns. He hadn't ridden a motorcycle in ages, and he was more than a little cautious as a result. That also made things a bit dicier at times. Eventually they made it back to the house okay. By that point it was early evening.

The rest of the family would be home soon. Pops would be going for his evening swim as the others debated the best course of action for dinner.

But for now, no one was around to observe as Will helped Jen make her way into the house and up the stairs to her bedroom. Had any of the cousins been there, he could only imagine the arched eyebrows and back and forth glances that would have been lobbed around the room.

The door to Jen's room opened with a creak, tilting inward to reveal her unmade bed. She'd never been one to worry about those things. Yet now, seeing the sheets pulled back, the pillows tossed where she'd left them that morning, Will felt even more like he was intruding, or crossing some line he shouldn't be approaching, not after all these years, not given her current situation.

Will walked Jen to the bed, sat on the edge beside her, and slowly leaned her back across the sheets. She moaned softly, and gingerly crawled across the bed toward the pillows. Will couldn't help but wonder if she even knew he was there.

He stood and watched to see if she'd open her eyes again, but she merely sighed and hugged her pillow tight. He stepped out into the hall, closing the door behind him, where he waited for another beat in case the noise of the door stirred her. When all remained quiet, he headed down the stairs to the front hallway, and was just taking the last step when Sara walked around the corner and saw him. His face must have frozen in a guilty expression, as she immediately gave him a knowing look.

"What'cha doin'?"

"Nothing," he said. "I was just helping Jen to bed."

"Oh *really?*" Sara countered. "Isn't it a little early?"

Will looked at her blankly as the words failed to come.

"Relax, Will. I'm just messing with you," Sara said. "Things cool?"

"I'm... not so sure." Will answered.

Then he noticed his younger cousin's rather decked out look. If he didn't know better, he'd have thought she was heading out for the night.

"Where are you off to?"

"I got a date. Guy I met last night. Real cutie. Real French."

Will started for the kitchen. "I won't hold you then. Have a good time."

He turned to walk away, but noticed Sara didn't budge.

"Are you sure you're okay?" she asked.

"Yeah!"

"Well, don't do anything I wouldn't do," Sara said.

"I was just about to tell you the same thing."

"Shit. Then we're both in trouble." Sara smiled. "Later cuz."

She stepped out the door and was gone.

~

Will tore off a piece of baguette, smeared some room temperature brie over it, and headed out to the pool, where he found Pops spread out on the chaise, flipping through Nekos' copy of *The Da Vinci Code.*

Pops looked up at him and raised the book. "Will, you read this yet?"

"Nah, I'm more of a Stephen King guy."

"It's a great big pile of crap, but hell if I can't put it down."

Will laughed. "Yeah?"

"Yeah," his grandfather answered. He dropped the book and looked off across the pool forlornly. "Ohhhhhh....shit..."

Will laughed again. "What?"

"I don't have a clue what to get your grandmother for our anniversary."

"I'm sure she doesn't care, Pops. Whatever you get her will mean a lot."

Pops stared at him with a look of sheer disbelief. "Do you even *know* your grandmother?" he asked. "It will matter all right! It has to be just right. No sentimental horse shit. Just something that says 'you're the one' in a dignified, tasteful, but show-stopping way. You know, the impossible."

"You really don't have any ideas?"

Pops shook his head. "Not a one."

"Would you like some help?" Will said.

"I sure as hell would."

"Then why don't we go looking?"

* * *

Jen was lying on her side, drifting in and out of sleep when she heard the vans pull up in the gravel drive, and the cousins' voices ululating in through the windows.

She heard Karen and Lucy walk in the front door and head into the kitchen. It was amazing the way sounds echoed off the tile floors and plaster walls.

"Awful quiet," Lucy mused. "Where did everybody go?"

There was a pause and the shuffling of feet, then Karen said.

"It looks like your father went downtown with Will."

~

The sun was setting as Will and his grandfather made their way through the booths of artists by the water. Rather than delving into the shops, Pops, in his typical fashion, had proposed they pick up some gelato and stroll by the water. While they walked, he'd told Will the story of how he and Karen had met.

"OK, so that's how you guys *met*," Will interjected. "But how did you *get together*?"

"I wore her down. 'I wouldn't say that to her face either, but she knows. We were classmates, and we were friends, but I always wanted it to be something more. It just never seemed like it was meant to be. Then we graduated, and I enlisted and went over seas, and of course, that's when things changed."

"You wrote her?"

Pops nodded. "And she wrote me. A lot. And then we got together in New York."

"Together?" Will said with an arched eyebrow.

Pops gave him a look that let Will know he was ignoring the insinuation. "Then I got out of the service, and the rest is history."

"So what changed? You lived right across the hall from each other for years, then you're thousands of miles away and she sees what you've been getting at?"

189

Pops shrugged. "Hell if I know. The heart is one hell of a fickle muscle. It always wants what it can't have, but occasionally, it finds a way to get those things anyway. If there's one thing you can count on, it's that nothing ever works out how you think it will. Or *should* for that matter. But in retrospect, it always seems right somehow."

~

The light was all but gone when she awoke again. Jen once more heard tires on the gravel drive. Only this time the noise was different, more guttural. The sound of a motorcycle.

Will.

She remembered the ride home from the port.

Will's grandmother called across the front yard.

"There you boys are. We're just heading downtown for dinner if you're interested."

"Oh yeah," Pops called back.

Then she heard Will.

"I'm not feeling one hundred percent actually," he said. "I may sit this one out."

"Oh, that's too bad," Karen replied. "Are you sure?"

He must have nodded, because Jen didn't hear any more discussion, but she could just make out the muffled footsteps as the three of them disbursed and someone, Will she assumed, walked around the side of the house alone.

Jen sighed and rolled over onto her stomach. She looked across the bed, and for the first time spotted James' forgotten Blackberry sitting on the nightstand.

Her eyes narrowed.

It felt like weeks since he had left for New York.

She reached her hand across the bed, and ran her fingers down his pillow and over the wrinkled sheets. Then she reached further, her fingertips stretching out for the phone, just brushing against the plastic, and with a quick swipe, she knocked it off the table. It disappeared from sight, followed by the soft, satisfying crackle of breaking plastic.

~

The sounds of bullfrogs filled the air as Jen walked across the lawn, her eyes locked on the light shining from Will's window. A breeze whispered through the trees, raising goose bumps on her arms and legs as she approached the edge of the pool. She hesitated, unsure if the cool air had set her heart racing, or whether it was the thrill of anticipation. Everything about the evening had a forbidden sensation, yet she couldn't seem to talk herself out of what she was about to do. What she was *determined* to do. The mere thought of *not* acting on her feelings, seemed to drive her forward with greater intensity.

She stared down into the rippling water. Then the air grew still, and the waves on the pool's surface rippled away to the far corners, stretching the water as smooth as glass, and in that moment of calm, she made up her mind. Without a second thought, she turned in the direction of the guesthouse and started up the stairs to Will's room.

Will had begged out of dinner that night, instead grabbing some more bread and cheese from the kitchen, and absconding with a bottle of rosé from the pantry. He was in no mood to deal with strangers, or restaurant staff, or family. What he wanted more than anything was the chance to be alone, to sort out the strange surge of old feelings that had resurfaced over the last two days. He stood in the middle of the room, drinking from a glass of wine, which he had filled quite generously, almost to the top. He tipped the glass back, took a last long gulp, then wiped his mouth on his shirtsleeve, set the glass on the bedside table, and walked across the room, pulling his shirt over his head as he headed for the bathroom. He was just about to strip out of his remaining clothes and head into the shower, when he heard the creak of door hinges, and turned to see Jen standing in the main doorway.

She was giving him a funny look.

And she looked *good*.

"Hey," she said softly.

He swallowed and took a breath.

"Hey."

Jen ran her fingertips back through her hair, brushed it behind one ear nervously, then she looked up at him with an expression he remembered all too well, and delivered his own words back to him.

"Do you remember how we used to-"

Will swallowed

"I remember," he said.

No sooner had he uttered the words, than she was moving towards him. Stepping in front of him. Setting her hands on his shoulders, and running them down his sides to his waist. She pulled him forward as he brought his hands up to the back of her neck, and drew her towards him. They kissed, hands gliding over warm skin, fingers swimming through hair. Lips warm, and light, and determined. Then they were falling back onto the bed, and, without a thought that they shouldn't, without a moment to decide, they began. And time, and the years, and all of their disagreements, whatever they might have been, fell away as they moved and whispered and laughed the way they had all those years ago. In another life.

~

They lay awake afterwards, looking up at the ceiling as the night sounds drifted in from outside. Jen rolled away from him, looking towards the window. Will rolled in the opposite direction. After a moment he turned back, pressing his body against her back as he pulled her against him.

"Was that a mistake?" he asked.

"No," she whispered.

He held her for minutes, or hours, until their eyes grew heavy, their eyelids drooped, and they slept.

* * *

The days that followed seemed to run in and out of one another. Hours together in Will's room.

Talking. Laughing.

Then saying nothing. Just the sound of their breathing, and their thoughts.

When they weren't slipping away by themselves, they went

to the beach with the family. Went to dinner in the same restaurants and vineyards as Will's relatives, but they might just have well have been alone.

The cousins watched. And they whispered. And Jen and Will took their whispered comments and glances in stride. Saw them, understood them even, but never once felt an impulse to acknowledge or explain anything.

It was clear that they knew. Knew whatever there was to know.

And it was just as clear that it bothered them.

And for whatever reason, Jen and Will couldn't have cared less.

As the days moved on, and the patterns grew, they slowly drew away from the crowd, took longer, more frequent daytrips to the villages and vineyards on their own, just the two of them aboard Jeff Pepper's bike.

They took the motorcycle off road, kicking up dusty trails among the rows of grapes, parking the bike among the vines, and walking through the rows, til they found a place to eat lunch, and drink wine, and kiss.

Eventually, they stopped joining the family for every meal, and found restaurants outside of town, farther and farther removed from the crowd, and the need to conceal their feelings.

They ate alone on ageless stone patios that looked out to the ocean. They drank rosé, and they talked about the past, and the future, and anything but what they were doing and how long it would last.

And always, they returned home, to the house, to Will's

room, where once again, as they had every night before, they would close the door, slip into bed, and lose themselves in time and one another's arms.

~

A week later, they took the bike out of town, and wound their way up the winding roadways that led to the hilltop village of Grimaud. They passed the old cemetery, and drove over the stone roadways, until they found a quiet lookout where they parked the bike and began walking.

Eventually, they found their way to the ancient Roman Ruins at the town's highest point, where they made their way up into the ancient structures, and leaned against the stone walls, looking out over the town, over the red tile roofs, towards the ocean, where the sky was beginning to turn pink with the setting sun.

For a long while neither of them said anything. Then Will glanced down and saw a crushed beer can on the ground between his feet. For some reason, this struck him as funny.

He laughed, which drew Jen's attention.

"What so funny?"

"Good to see that even here, the kids sneak off to the ruins to drink beers."

"What do you think it's like to grow up in a place like this?"

"I don't know," Will mused. "I mean, when you grow up with a Roman ruin in your backyard, you've gotta have a sense of time and history."

"Like tradition?"

"No, more like scale. You probably think, 'Fuck tradition, I don't have a lot of time to make my mark.' You know you're just a blip in time; the brief fallout from your old man getting his rocks off."

"You have such a romantic world view," Jen muttered.

"You know I'm kidding," Will said. "I just mean that if you grow up here, you probably realize that a lot of the stuff you're told is important, really isn't."

"You think kids here have any fun?"

"Sure, and they probably don't even worry about it. What's the point? They sure don't *seem* to worry about things as much. 'Course, how much fun could they really be having? No one here ever buys my records, so they can't be having too good a time."

"Yeah. Your voice is the ultimate aphrodisiac, Will."

"You don't seem to mind," he answered.

"Spare me."

She grew quiet for a moment.

"What are we doing here?" she asked finally.

"I don't know. What do you want us to be doing?"

She shrugged. "Are we serious, or is this all some sort of self destructive fling? Just totally fucking everything up so it never happens again?"

"I don't think that's what it is." He looked her in the eyes. "I think we're being serious this time."

"You know I've gotta go back to New York."

"That's fine," Will replied. "I've got a place there."

"You do?"

"Yeah, I just bought it last-" He stopped suddenly, looking

confused for a moment. "Or wait, maybe I bought it two years ago. Geez, now that I think about it, there's a strong chance I have *two* places in the city. I'd better talk to Bobby about that."

Jen stared at him blankly, not sure if he was kidding.

"What about James, do we tell him?"

"We've got to, otherwise, my dear sweet cousins will do it for us."

"How do you think that will go?" Jen asked apprehensively.

"That is going to go... very, *very* badly."

Jen sighed heavily and Will pulled her against him.

"Think European," he said. "Just think European."

* * *

The vans were both gone when they returned to the house that night. The motorcycle's lone headlight panned across the front of the house, like a spotlight searching for escaped prisoners. Or witnesses.

Will pulled the bike up along the edge of the gravel driveway and cut the engine. He kicked the bike up on its stand and the two of them headed for the house. When they got to the large wooden front door, no one had thought to leave the light on, so they were forced to grope around in the dark, looking for the handle and trying to fit the key in the lock. Will had just managed to slip the old metal key into place, when Jen brought her hand up and placed it over his. Her thin fingers were cool to the touch. She moved in closer, and kissed him on the mouth, slowly. He brushed her hair behind one ear, and kissed the small patch of soft, warm skin between her jawbone and her neck.

Then he reached for the lock and fumbled with the key, eager to get inside. The door opened with a creak. They entered the hallway. It looked as though someone had left a light on in the kitchen.

"Want some wine?" Will asked.

"I don't need it, but sure."

They slipped into the kitchen, where Will walked over to the cabinet and took out two wine glasses. He pulled the cork from a half open bottle of rosé that he found sitting in an ice bucket on the counter. The group must have had their ritual bottle of chilled wine, then started a second, before they headed downtown.

Jen rummaged through the fridge, looking for something to eat.

"What do we have to choose from tonight?" Will asked.

"We've got leftover paté, a half-dozen croissants, and one crusty baguette," Jen said as she stood up straight and walked to the middle of the room. "Think we can make something from that?"

Will turned his back on her as he poured the rosé. Jen stood and watched him, her own back turned to the doorway.

"I think we can make do," Will said as he picked up the glasses and turned to hand one to Jen. "We can just have a bite to eat and-"

He stopped short as a figure stepped into the doorway behind her.

James.

"Hey, guys." James looked as though he'd just woken up.

He must have been sleeping on the living room couch.

Will and Jen were both taken aback, but Jen seemed to find her breath first.

"Hey," she said in a soft voice, almost a whisper.

James stepped forward and took her hand. He moved in for a kiss, but she turned her head at the last moment, took a half step to the right, and gave him an off balance hug.

From the corner of her eye, Jen could see Will watching. He turned away, and she diverted her gaze. Avoiding eye contact.

This was going to be difficult.

* * *

Some muttered excuses and a series of explanations, all painfully free of eye contact or inflection, got Jen and James upstairs. Alone, in what had been "their" room.

Jen stood at the foot of the bed as James unpacked his things.

She twisted her fingers together anxiously.

"How was the flight over?" she asked.

"A little bumpy, but not bad," he replied as he held a pair of rolled up socks in each hand, appearing to weigh them, like the lady of blind justice or something. Finally, he opened the bottom drawer of the armoire and tossed them in.

In the next movement, James crossed the room and gave her an awkward kiss.

"How were things here?" he asked.

She watched him warily, aching to see if he would sense something was amiss.

"They were okay."

He looked at her a moment, and gave her a funny expression.

"Gotten a little more comfortable with the family?"

She hesitated before she answered.

"Oh, you know, maybe a bit."

"Good, cause if we want to make this official, that will certainly make things easier."

Jen walked to the window and looked out across the yard. "Official?"

"You know- merge the assets."

Jen was silent

James walked over, set a hand on her shoulder, and lowered his head to look her in the eyes. "That was a joke, Jen."

"Yeah, I know," she said. "Guess I'm just not ready to joke about it."

"Are you ready to talk about it?"

"About what? Getting married?"

James seemed a bit irritated now. "Yeah, among other things."

"Sure. Yeah-" she said, and immediately knew the tone was wrong.

James dropped his hand from her shoulder and walked back over to the bed, where he half-heartedly took more clothes from his suitcase.

"What's up?" he asked finally.

"Nothings up," she replied as she walked into the bathroom and pulled her swimsuit down from the showerhead.

"Where are you going?"

"I'm going for a swim."

James stood in the middle of the room, holding a pink polo shirt in one hand. He watched her walk out of the room, then stood alone for a moment afterward, before he bunched up the shirt and threw it on the bed. Across the yard, he could hear his brother strumming his guitar in the guesthouse, and could almost smell the aroma of cigarette smoke wafting through the air and in through the window.

* * *

Lucy was sitting in a chair on the back lawn, looking out over the yard and sketching in a notebook when Karen sat down beside her, a mug of coffee in her hands.

"Good morning, mother." Lucy said.

"Good morning," Karen said as she glanced down at her daughter's notebook. "Very nice."

Karen sat and took a sip of her coffee. "I see James got back last night."

"That's what it looks like."

"Any idea which of the boys she stayed with?" Karen said.

Lucy stopped sketching and looked at her.

"That's something I try not to think about. And I *certainly* didn't think *you* had picked up on that."

"Of course I did," Karen replied. "I'm old, but I'm still a woman. I can tell when something is going on between two people, especially when one is my grandson."

"They're both your grandsons," Lucy said flatly.

"I know that, but with she and James..." Karen shrugged,

"There's nothing *there*."

"And what do you think about that?"

"The bigger question is what do *you* think about it?" her mother countered.

"What can I say? I know my sons. James might think he loves her, but at the same time, it's more likely that he's just looking to cross something off his "to-do list." If this relationship doesn't work, he'll just try for another solution."

"And Will?"

"Will is trying to figure things out, same as always, and his heart will get torn up if it doesn't work between the two of them this time."

"So you want her to go with Will?"

" I think she's the one for him. She always has been. If she wants the same thing, and it will make them happy, then yeah, that's what I'm hoping for."

~

Jen was lying on top of the covers as James got dressed in the bathroom. He stepped out, brushed his hands over the front of his shirt, and held up his arms.

"This look okay?"

Jen nodded.

"So, the anniversary dinner is at which restaurant?" James asked.

"One of the vineyards."

"You been there yet?"

She and Will had been there two nights earlier.

"Yeah," Jen replied cautiously. "Not with the whole family,

but it's nice."

James walked back into the bathroom, but continued speaking from the other room.

"Sixty years! Can you imagine being married to someone for sixty years?"

Jen rolled over and glanced at the new Blackberry on the bedside table.

"No," she said. "I can't."

"You gonna get ready?"

"In a minute. I'm just thinking."

~

The cousins were abustle as they stood on the front patio, touching up their makeup and glancing at their phones.

Peri walked out the front door, looked around, then tilted her head back and shouted, "Buses are moving out!"

Even from where she was standing in the back yard, Jen could hear Peri shouting. She took a drag from her cigarette and exhaled deeply as Will walked around the corner.

He looked upset but determined as he shook his head and squared his jaw.

"I'm bowing out," he said to her. "I'm bowing out."

"Now you're the one saying everything twice," Jen replied, but she struggled to find the right words to say next.

The car horn again blasted out front.

"We have to go," she said.

"Hold on-"

"They *will* leave without us you know."

Will held up two sets of car keys, jingled them between

them.

"They'll have to wait."

Jen looked from the keys, to Will, and down to her feet.

"We'll talk," she said.

"Who? You and me, or you and James?"

"You and me! *And* James! I don't know!"

Jen finished her cigarette, scratched the butt out on the stucco wall, and walked away.

~

This was one of the trendier locales in Saint Tropez.

Candlelit tables surrounded a crystal clear pool that glowed under the night sky. Music played softly in the background as groups dined at the various tables.

James sat at one end of the family's table, rolling a ring case in his fingers underneath the tablecloth.

Pops clinked his water glass with a fork. "Everyone. Everyone," He declared as he rose to his feet. "I've said it before, but I just want to tell you again how happy I am to have all of you here with Karen and myself to celebrate this big day. It means a lot, it really does."

The family nodded and raised their glasses of rosé as Pops continued.

"I never would have thought that I'd be standing here today, this far down the line, with this woman, and this family, and trust me, I know I'm getting sentimental and disgusting, and I know that there will be much more to come, but I just feel very fortunate at the moment, and I wanted to take this opportunity to appreciate what I have here. Thank you all again."

Pops hurried to raise his glass and nodded happily, if ever so misty-eyed, as the group toasted and drank.

James looked around the table as he sipped from his glass. Then he set it down and rose to his feet.

Will rolled up his napkin and set it before him.

Jen just looked uneasy.

"On that note," James began. "I just want to say congratulations to Pops and Gammy and say how happy I am that the two of you got together all those years ago, because if you hadn't, none of us would have gotten to enjoy, well, all of this-"

James swept his arm around the table, as the majority of the family smiled and nodded. Will and Jen looked pained as James plowed ahead.

"So, along that line of thinking, and after a lot of soul-searching, I'd like to see if I can help begin the next chapter of this family's history-"

The table suddenly buzzed to life with small rustles of movement and nervous fidgeting from every corner.

Lucy whispered under her breath to Karen, "Ohhhh my-"

"*God*," her mother finished.

The cousins pulled their hands to their mouths in nervous excitement.

"I know I haven't always been the easiest guy to deal with," James mused. "And romance isn't always my forte. But, Jen-"

Jen looked panicked. Her eyes locked on Will. James looked from Jen to Will, and began to stammer.

"Jen, I-"

He looked at Will, whose expression sagged.

A pinched smile passed over James' face as the pieces fell together.

He almost laughed as he took a step back and turned to Will with a murderous expression. "You *son of a bitch*. I knew it. I just *knew* it."

"James, not here, man," Will said.

James almost sat down, then he stopped, threw his napkin down on the ground, and stepped towards Will.

"What the hell was I thinking? There were a couple of blind items in *The Post* last week, but I told myself it was someone else, or some sort of misunderstanding. I thought *nah, he's my brother, he wouldn't do that. Not even him-*"

Will looked around the restaurant, then up and down their own table. "James, not here, please."

"Why did you do it?" James muttered.

"Why did *you?*" Will shot back.

"Boys!" Pops shouted.

"Do you just need to wrap things up once and for all, is that it?" James asked.

Pops whipped his head around. "James!"

James slowly moved closer. Getting in his younger brother's face now. He lurched forward, grabbed ahold of Will's shirt, pulled him forward, then shoved him away. Hard.

Will remained passive. "James-" he started.

But James was running at him now. Grabbing at the collar of Will's shirt as Will wrapped his arms around his brother's chest and tried to lock him down. They struggled in an awkward bear hug for a moment as the family looked on in shock.

The two of them pushed and pulled and shoved each other back and forth until James got an arm free and took a swipe at Will, who grabbed James by the lapels, swung him around, and shoved him backwards toward the pool. But James wasn't giving in, and he threw his arm over Will's shoulder, pulling him down with him as he lost his balance. In a flurry of waving arms and legs, the two brothers plunged into the restaurant's pool.

Pops walked over to the pool as his grandsons bobbed to the surface. He looked around the restaurant, only to catch sight of the last two people he wanted to see, especially at a time like this.

There, across the pool, wine glasses held aloft, scowls more pronounced than *ever,* sat the German couple.

Pops looked at the disapproving observers, then he clenched his teeth and reached out his arms to pull his grandsons to the edge of the pool.

"Congratulations boys, you've turned this into an episode of *Dynasty.*"

Will climbed out of the water, his clothes dripping. James followed close behind. The two of them stood beside each other, arms and legs spread wide, water pooling around their feet.

James looked at Jen without a word. He took the dripping ring case from his pocket, flipped the lid open, and pulled the ring from the wet velvet lining. "The hell with it," he said, as he tossed it into the water and walked away.

A lone gasp rang from the cousins' end of the table as Peri pushed her chair back and jumped to her feet. She walked to the edge of the pool, looked down into the water, and dove head first after the ring.

-

The vans pulled up to the house, their arrivals staggered by Nekos and Pops, who had split driving duties and instinctively realized that the longer the lag between arrivals – with Will in one car and James in the other – the better.

The cousins all slipped away as soon as the front door was unlocked. The adults stood in the kitchen, exchanging looks, before they too retreated to their rooms.

James marched into the house and up the stairs. A door slammed.

Will stood in the front hallway and turned to Jen as she walked inside.

"Jen-"

She shook her head and looked away. "Not now, Will."

Then she too walked up the stairs, visibly nervous, leaving Will alone in the hallway to listen to the sounds of Jen and James' rising voices. Will ran his fingers through his hair, walked out to the patio, and lit a cigarette. The smoke swirled in the chilled air around him, then trailed behind as he slipped his hands in his pockets and trudged off in the direction of the pool house.

~

A taxi was waiting in the driveway when Will got up the next morning. He heard the engine idling as he crossed the yard and peaked out the kitchen window as he poured his cup of coffee. A few moments later, James walked from the front of the house to the car, his luggage in hand. Will watched the driver load his brother's bags into the trunk, but he couldn't see any of Jen's things.

Was that a good sign? He was trying to picture a scenario in which she'd stay behind with him if James left.

He took a sip of his coffee and leaned against the counter as he heard the taxi drive away.

Sara walked into the room looking *much* the worse for wear. The two of them sized each other up, wordlessly attempting to determine which of them looked shittier. It was clearly a draw, so Will took it upon himself to break the silence.

"What are you doing home so early? Where's prince charming?"

"He had to go back to Paris," Sara answered. "His wife was having the baby."

"Charming."

"Isn't it?"

They sat in silence for a moment, then Will reached for a stale croissant, took a bite, and let the crumbs tumble from his mouth.

He sighed.

"What are your plans for the day?" Sara asked.

"Nothing. Thought I'd wait until Jen got up. See how she's doing after last night.

Sara looked up suddenly. "You don't know?"

He looked away as his eyes tingled.

"She's gone, isn't she?"

"She took a cab to the airport last night."

Will started to speak, then stopped. He looked up at the ceiling, then over at Sara.

"Well in that case, I guess my schedule is pretty free."

Sara didn't say anything in response. She just walked over to him and gave him a hug.

"There's no saying what will happen, Will."

Somehow, he wasn't so sure that was true. He'd have to get through the rest of the week alone in Saint Tropez. And though he might try to slip away to some of the spots he and Jen had been visiting together over the last few days, he wasn't sure if being with his family and *feeling* alone would be better or worse than returning to those places and *knowing* that he was.

New York

He could hear them out in the darkness again.

Murmuring.

Waiting for his return.

It had been too long since they'd played. The weather had cooled. The holidays were coming. And here he was again. Back in New York City.

As they were wont to do, the band was teasing their instruments behind him. Filling the air with an anticipatory cacophony of sound.

He turned to the crowd and was met with the sounds of wild cheering.

"Thank you very much everybody," he said. "It's good to be back. *Good* to be back."

Then a lone voice shouted for *Mischief Night*. And a moment later the crowd picked up the call. Will cocked his head at an angle as they continued. Then he shook his head from side to side.

"Come on y'all. If you're good maybe, *maybe* I'll give you a little update on that number."

The crowd cheered.

"But I'm not gonna play it," he continued.

The crowd booed and Will glanced at the band, then back to the audience.

"This is a tough crowd tonight. How about this? What if I play you a new one. Something totally fresh. First time performed anywhere."

Then they were cheering. *Roaring.*

"Sound good?" Will asked. "See sometimes- just sometimes, you gotta take a little break from something. Try something new. So I'm gonna be putting that particular song aside for a while. You understand, right?"

The sound of the crowd picked up. They were ready for him to play now, so he'd have to tease them a little longer.

He stared into the spotlight and tried his best not to look offstage. Not yet anyway.

"This next song, this next song is about somebody from once upon a time, who I really cared about. We crossed paths again not too long ago. And although I had been, for want of better terms, a right *asshole* back in the day... time and forgiveness heal all wounds. And now, now things are going great guns, if you know what I mean... And I hope you do!"

He couldn't wait anymore.

"I'm still working on a title, but I kinda like the sound of *Rosé in Saint Tropez.* That sorta has a nice ring to it, doesn't it?"

Finally, he looked into the darkness offstage. He could just make her out. Standing off in the shadows.

"Course, maybe that sounds like some hoity toity Joan Collins *bullshit*, you know, so I've kinda been thinking of something shorter."

Then a flash of light from the stage swirled past her and she stepped forward.

"I think I'd kinda like to call this song that I'm about to play, maybe not *Rosé in Saint Tropez*, but... *Jennifer.*"

That's when Jen stepped out of the shadows. She looked over at Will, brushing her hair from her forehead nervously. She smiled at him, and he smiled back.

"So, what do you say we give this new number a shot and see how things go, see how it all works out this time around?"

Jen nodded in embarrassment as the crowd roared their approval and the band started rolling out a feverishly hyper and distinctly upbeat buildup.

The lights flashed.

The crowd danced.

Will looked at Jen, and then, after all these years, he sang her a song.

Mike Attebery is the author of the novels On/Off, Billionaires Bullets Exploding Monkeys, Seattle On Ice, and Bloody Pulp. He lives in Seattle, Washington with his wife and daughter. He is currently at work on his sixth novel.

www.mikeattebery.com

www.ingramcontent.com/pod-product-compliance
Lightning Source LLC
Chambersburg PA
CBHW061925130726
47909CB00012B/1016